GENTLY DOES IT!

The cast of characters in Adrian Stoll's life could have come from any of his sensational movies. A beautiful mistress whose live-in contract was about to expire. A stunning starlet with no morals. A cynical scriptwriter with no scruples. A shady financier with no capital. A jealous cousin who wanted everything Adrian possessed.

Each of them had a motive for murder. One of them had taken the part of killer and played it to perfection. But when the curtain came down on this real-life drama, the ingenious Inspector Gently would be waiting in the wings. . . .

Murder Ink® Mysteries

Scene Of The Crime® Mysteries

A Scene Of The Crime® Mystery

GENTLY THROUGH the WOODS

Alan Hunter

A DELL BOOK

Published by
Dell Publishing Co., Inc.
1 Dag Hammarskjold Plaza
New York, New York 10017

GENTLY THROUGH THE WOODS was originally published
under the title GENTLY IN TREES
by Cassell & Company, Ltd., London.

Dell ® TM 681510, Dell Publishing Co., Inc.

ISBN: 0-440-13055-7

Reprinted by arrangement with Macmillan Publishing Co., Inc.

Printed in the United States of America

First Dell printing—June 1982

For Julian & Kathleen Symons

The characters and events in this book are fictitious, the locale is sketched from life.

1

The Volkswagen Dormobile entered Latchford by the London road, turned right into the town centre, and selected the road to Cross. Nobody noticed it, particularly. Caravettes were common enough, at the end of June. It was latish on a Saturday evening, about the time when campers departed from the town and returned to their sites. The Volks was newish, but not otherwise remarkable; Neptune Blue, with a white elevating roof. In the rear, over the engine compartment, was packed some photographic equipment, but this was not obvious from outside. So the Volks puttered through the narrow streets and away without anyone noticing it, to remember.

It went down by the Castle Hill, which rose grassy and dim against the evening afterglow, then crossed the River Latch by a humpy bridge, near which drizzled the weir of some vanished mill. Then there was a junction of two A roads. The Volkswagen selected its course unhesitatingly. It puttered along self-intently, letting the impatient flash and go by. Not that there were many cars, that evening—Cross, after all, was just another small town; and Latchford itself reached only to the river: the road then passed into empty, healthy country. Northwards lay the wilderness of the Battle Area, with its ghostly shells of villages, and southwards breckland and starving fields, where the poor soil was snowed with chalky flints.

Ancient country, still breathing prehistory. Few people had lived there, since the Iceni. And into it, into the twilight, puttered the unremarkable Volkswagen.

Came to trees. At first, broken lines of them; twisty, indigenous Scots pines. Looking deformed, almost, so low and twisted, with dark, bowed, shaggy crowns. Beggar-trees, old and cunning, who had watched the centuries come and go; old men of the heath. They reached out stealthily, fingering for the Volks as it passed below. But the Volks cared nothing. And ahead, like darkness, spread an arboreal company of a different character: trees tall, and trees straight, shouldering together in massive unity. The road bored towards them, full of aggression, but then lost heart and swung right; leaving a minor road behind for those bold enough to meet such trees. The Volks flicked on its light, flashed, and turned into the minor road, without pausing. Passing, as it did so, a discreet sign worded: FORESTRY COMMISSION / LATCH-FORD CHASE.

The twilight was heavy here, in the long, deep aisle of the forest. On each side of the road ran a grass verge, overhung with monster oaks and beeches. And behind these, the pines. There they brooded, in solid night. Divided, every so often, by murky rides, each signed with a white, stencilled number. And all silent, with tree silence. Nothing but the burble of the Volks. No sign of bird, or moth, or the roe deer that were said to roam here. Empty, silent, but charged with presence: the forest seemed to hold its breath.

The lights of the Volks picked up a fresh sign: WARREN RIDE / 2 KILOMETRES. The sign was painted on a slab of timber, crosscut from a felled tree. Then came the ride itself, a junction left, with a similar sign, on a grassed island; and here the Volks slowed, giving no signal, and clambered over ruts into the ride. The surface was rough, though there was a surface, distinguishing this ride from its neighbours; a marly, stony surface, with outcrops of chalk, stained reddish with iron. And this ride was wider: had one deep grass verge, say fifty feet to the trees; compartments of fifty-year pine, Scots and Corsican, edged with small beeches, larches and maples. So it was lighter, too, having a strip of sky. Yet the Volks bumbled cautiously along the track. Thick, reddish dust, not yet laid by dew, spurted from its wheels, and left a haze behind it.

Another kilometre—then the Volks halted, and the driver switched on the light in his cab. He was puzzling over something he held in his hand: too small for a map, more like a pamphlet. Where he had stopped was near the end of the ride, where it opened up into a partly cleared glade: a picnic area, like as not, though the light was too dim to make it out. Anyway, the driver got down and switched a torch along the verges. It settled at last on a short stake, or post, driven into the ground near the junction with a cross-ride. The driver approached it. The top of the stake had been sawn across in a half-wedge, and into this surface had been carved two arrowheads, one painted yellow, one blue. Both pointed down the cross-ride. The driver switched off his torch, returned to the Volks and climbed in. He restarted the engine, wheeled the van round, and drove very slowly into the cross-ride.

The going here was rather more suited to Forestry Land-Rovers than caravettes—drifts of pine-needles, lumping ribs of chalk, and gulches of red mud. But the Volks handled it firmly, delicately raising and lowering its separately suspended wheels, its boxer engine chaffering happily as the throttle was pressed and eased. The ride was narrow, also winding—unlike the other rides in the forest. To the right it skirted Douglas pines, to the left some truly gigantic Scots.

On this side, too, it was fenced with steel mesh, with rabbit-netting at the foot; and behind the fence grew bramble and underbrush, concealing whatever lay beyond. Then, a gate. The Volks halted. Its driver sat some moments, staring. The gate was of metal, as tall as the fence, and clad with sections of mesh and the rabbit netting. None of it new, except the rabbit-netting. A rusty chain and padlock secured it. Attached to it was a notice: WD PROPERTY / KEEP OUT / UNEXPLODED BOMBS.

Once more, the driver switched on his cab-light and consulted his map or pamphlet. A little doubtfully, he got down with his torch and searched along the fence beyond the gate. What he found this time was a small contraption, made partly of wood and partly of sheet-metal, let into the fence and the rabbit-netting, just by a gap in the underbrush. It seemed to decide him. He came swiftly back to the gate and gave the rusty padlock a jerk. The padlock opened; he showed no surprise, but pushed back the gate and drove in. Then he closed the gate again, though without replacing the padlock.

And now the Volks was in virtual bush-country, tramping on bramble, bracken and snowberry, with the rusty boles of the pines lurching massively through its headlights. But its destination was close: grumbling over a bank, it wallowed down into a small clearing, free of the underbrush; a tiny dell, where nothing grew except meagre grass, nettles and campion. The driver levelled the Volks, and parked. He cut the engine, but not the lights. What they rested on, across the dell, was a beech tree of curious form. From a massive root-base it had sent up four stems, the boughs from which had intergrown, so that there were several complete arches of live timber, and others in the process of forming. But it was not this phenomenon that interested the driver. His attention was focused on the base of the tree. There, among the roots, and partly concealed by nettles, lay the shadowy entrance of an excavated tunnel.

The man acted quickly but silently. He went round to the side-door of the caravette. From the rear compartment he took apparatus which he set up close to the beech. Returning, he plugged in a cable, switched on the apparatus, switched off his headlights. Now there was a soft, brilliant white light, flooding the ground in front of the tunnel. The man donned headphones. He sat in the doorway, another piece of apparatus resting in his lap.

Some time later, soft as a cat, he raised this piece of apparatus to his cheek.

'Do you think he's coming?' Edwin Keynes said, resting his whisky glass on his knee.

'Oh yes,' Maryon Britton replied. 'He's coming. If he doesn't arrive tonight, he will tomorrow.'

'Building the suspense,' Edwin grimaced.

'Well he *is* a professional,' Maryon said. She made a small, actressy mouth. 'You should know how he loves a production.'

Edwin nodded, ruefully. 'My dear cousin.'

'He'll have us all here in the lounge,' Maryon said. 'Then he'll make a brisk entrance, carrying his briefcase, march straight past us, and turn.' She sighed. 'Poor Adrian. Living with him has *always* been a production. I may have retired from the stage, but I'm always on a set when Adrian's around.'

Edwin chuckled. 'Is that how he makes love?'

Maryon sniffed. 'Something like that. Perhaps it's my fault. But I can't see it. You don't have any complaints, do you?'

'You know better,' Edwin said. He drank. 'But you must have loved him at one time.'

Maryon shook her head decidedly. 'No. I haven't that excuse, even.'

'Just a little?'

'Not at all. You may as well know the worst about me. I hooked on to Adrian for mercenary reasons. When it became clear I was a dud actress.'

'You're rationalizing,' Edwin said. 'I'm sure it wasn't like that at the time. I can remember you, you were full of high spirits—and Adrian strutting round you like a peacock. *He* wasn't in love, just vain as Lucifer. But you were thrilled enough, at first.'

'Just over-acting,' Maryon said.

'Ah-ah,' Edwin said. 'A genuine crush.'

'Yes, but it wasn't *love*,' Maryon said. 'I didn't *give* myself to him. It was just selfishly exciting to get hold of Adrian. After all, he does have good looks, and money, and a big reputation as a director. And he was still married to a star, then. It gave me a professional thrill to catch him.'

'You had feeling for him, Maryon.'

'No.'

'Now you're ashamed at having to admit it. You would sooner I thought you were a gold-digger than that you were even taken in by Adrian.'

'Utter bilge.'

'Because you're not really mercenary.'

She sent him a quizzical look: then smiled.

'In the world's eyes, anyway,' she said. 'I'm the image of a classic case. The actress who wasn't going to make it, and who hooked her director instead.' She looked glum. 'And how they'll crow now, all those lovely, beautiful people. The fool, that's me, didn't even insure. Because I could have married him, after the divorce.'

Edwin looked at her steadily. 'So why didn't you?'

'Just as I told you. I wasn't in love.'

'Yet you've stayed with him.'

'Why not? It's the easiest way of earning a living.'

She got up restlessly, an urgent figure, and poured herself a shot of Dubonnet: stood while she took the first sip, then returned to her seat. She gazed at the glass.

'That's not true, altogether. Like most motives, mine are mixed. For one thing I'm lazy, I stick in a groove. And for another, I had to educate Jenny. But principally—I don't know quite how to put this, not without sounding wretchedly smug—I felt vaguely sorry for Adrian. At the bottom, he's such an unhappy person.'

'Unhappy?' Edwin echoed doubtfully. 'Do you think the word has a meaning for Adrian?'

'Yes,' she nodded. 'I think it does. He's busy and successful, but still unhappy. There's something missing in him, some point of contact. He daren't let other people touch him. He's buried away inside himself, out of reach, quite alone.'

Edwin looked incredulous. 'And you. You reached him?'

'No. But I did know the problem existed. And he felt I knew, and it was important to him. I was the nearest he could get to a real contact.'

Edwin still looked unbelieving. 'Well, it is possible,' he granted. 'But all that's over now, in any case. He's seeking his soul in other quarters.'

'He won't find it there.'

'He won't find it ever. You were the best chance the idiot had.'

'Thank you for that, Edwin.' She sipped from the glass; and the glass had a slight tremor.

Edwin drank too. Outside it was dusk, and the cedar down the lawn stood blackly brooding. The scent of honeysuckle wafted through the French windows, and the scent of stock: the night air was warm. Inside, a single lamp was lit. The lounge was suffused with dulled shadows. Adrian's expensive furniture and pictures looked slightly oppressive, a well-dressed set. In the thick silence, one could hear the pipping of bats that hawked round the cedar.

'Have I made very much difference?' Edwin said, slowly.

'No,' she said. 'It was over before.'

'How long?'

Her shoulders moved. 'A long time. Before, anyway.'

'Does he know?'

'Not from me,' she said. 'But that's not to say he hasn't guessed. But it's all the same. He hasn't been near me for—oh, since Jenny went to the High School. He's probably had other women for that. Why not? I never bother him at the flat. He comes and goes. No—it's the money I lent you that sticks in his throat.'

'But that's paid back now. Thank heavens, I'm solvent.'

'Just the same, it sticks in his throat.'

Edwin nodded. 'And you're convinced he'll go through with it.'

'Yes, oh yes. It will be this weekend.'

'And then?'

She made another mouth.

'You must come to me,' Edwin said. 'There's room at the cottage, and room for Jennifer. Lawrence can sleep in his bit of a studio.'

Maryon didn't reply; she sat deep in the settee, her glass poised near her mouth. Her eyes were empty, distant. Sitting like that, she looked tenderly girlish.

'Maryon, I love you,' Edwin said suddenly.

She flashed him a smile. 'Yes. Tell me that.'

'I love you,' he said. 'And to hell with Adrian.'

She smiled again, strangely, and finished her drink.

But then there were steps on the gravel outside, and Maryon's daughter, Jennifer, entered. She was followed by Lawrence Turner, who was all beard and sensitive, large eyes. Jennifer looked moody. She had longer features than her mother and little of her mother's outgoing nature. Now she stared round the room peevishly, seeking for signs of an alien presence.

'So he hasn't come, then,' she said, grumpily.

'Oh, he may come yet,' her mother smiled.

'No,' Jennifer said. 'He won't come now. We shan't see His Highness tonight.'

'He could be latish,' Edwin said. 'I know he was directing today at Television Centre.'

'No,' Jennifer said stubbornly. 'He isn't coming. Nor tomorrow either. Not at all.'

'You odd girl!' Maryon said, surprised. 'How do *you* know he isn't coming? Lawrence, what's got into my daughter? What have you been up to this evening?'

Lawrence had faded into a distant chair. Now he flushed behind his beard.

'I don't know,' he said gruffly, nervously. 'She's been like it all evening.'

Jennifer stalked to the bar and poured herself a gin. She drank about half of it in a gulp. Then made a face.

'*He* wants to marry me,' she said. 'To take me away from the squalor I live in.'

Maryon raised her eyebrows. 'Is this true, Lawrence?'

'Well, it was mentioned,' Lawrence faltered. 'But we've been through all that before. I realize it isn't possible, yet.'

'No, I should think not,' Maryon said. 'You're too young and foolish, both of you. And you haven't sold a single picture, yet, Lawrence—at least, not to anyone except your friends. What a *stupid* idea.'

Lawrence blushed deeper. 'I wasn't suggesting doing

it tomorrow!' he said. 'And I don't see why it should upset Jenny. It wasn't something new I was springing on her.'

'Then why is she in a mood?'

'I don't know!' Lawrence blurted. 'We've been for a stroll round by the bridge. I haven't been able to say anything right.'

Edwin clicked his tongue sympathetically. 'We're all under a bit of strain,' he said. 'The axe is being sharpened for this weekend. Jenny was expecting to find Adrian here when she got back.'

Jennifer gulped the rest of her drink and came forward slowly to the centre of the room.

'But that's just the point,' she said. 'I *wasn't* expecting him. I *knew* he wouldn't be here.'

They all stared at her.

'But *how*?' Maryon said.

Jennifer shrugged her narrow shoulders. 'Oh, nothing I can tell you. Just a sort of sadness. I've been feeling it all day.' She dropped down suddenly on the sheepskin hearthrug, and sat with arms clasped round her knees. 'I guess I'm psychic, that's all. But I don't think Adrian is ever coming back here.'

'Just wishful thinking, my girl,' Maryon said. 'Adrian will never miss his big scene.'

'No,' Jennifer said. 'It isn't that at all, mums. I just can't explain the way I feel.' She twisted the belt of her jersey dress. 'Of course, I've been fed up with what's going to happen. I'm not like you, taking it as it comes. I can't *bear* the idea of him throwing us out. But this is different—I can't help myself. I'm suddenly terribly sad about Adrian. I look at this room, all the things of his in it, and I feel he's never coming back to them again. I don't *want* to feel sad—because I *hate* him! But I do, I can't help it.'

Silence for some moments. Jennifer sat staring.

'Well, it could be like that,' Edwin said, awkwardly. 'Perhaps Adrian felt he played his big scene last week, and that any encore would be an anticlimax. So now he is retiring into Olympian disdain. After all, his lawyers can take care of it.'

'Rubbish,' Maryon said promptly. 'That's not Adrian. Last week was only a curtain-raiser. He was setting us up for something, a real humdinger. He'd never let a lawyer steal his thunder.'

'He could be ill, or something.'

'Adrian's *never* ill.'

'Well, it can't have been an accident. We would have heard.'

'Too convenient, anyway,' Maryon said. She broke off, her eyes suddenly large. 'Oh, it's all rubbish!' she said. 'Jenny, you're an ass. You're not psychic, you're just eighteen.'

Jenny hugged her knees, saying nothing. But continuing to stare, all the same. Then the bracket-clock struck, in the corner, and Lawrence got hastily to his feet.

'I think I'll go,' he said. 'I need an early night.'

Nobody pressed him to change his mind. He paused in front of Jennifer; Jennifer ignored him. He ducked his head clumsily, and went. They heard his footsteps retreating.

'You're not serious about him, Jenny, are you?' Maryon said.

'Oh, I don't know,' Jennifer said broodingly. 'He isn't such a drag all the time.'

'But, my lamb, he's penniless.'

'So what are we?'

'That's *exactly* the point!' Maryon cried.

'Oh, hold on, now,' Edwin said. 'Lawrence has talent. He'll make the grade.'

'Anyway, you're too young,' Maryon fretted. 'My

goodness, just out of High School. And he doesn't
know what he wants either. You two are murder for
each other.'

Jennifer jumped up. 'Me too,' she said. 'I'm due
for an early night as well.'

'Wait!' Maryon cried. 'I want to *talk* to you!'

But Jennifer ran out of the room.

'Oh, wretched girl!' Maryon fumed. Then she
caught Edwin's eye. 'And you, you egg her on!' she
nagged. 'Oh, that girl needs a *father*!'

Edwin rocked his shoulders. He rose, stretched, and
went across to the French windows. Outside, now, it
was completely dark, with no moon in the heavy sky.
The cedar was invisible. But, behind it, the sable reef
of the Chase just etched a horizon.

Edwin closed the French windows and drew the
curtains.

'Do we take it he won't be coming?'

'Oh, I'm tired of thinking about it!' Maryon said.
'Nothing can change it. What will be, will be.'

Edwin came to the settee, where she sat, and stood
looking down at her for a moment. Then he dropped
down beside her, and laid his arm on her shoulders.

'It won't be so bad. I know I'm a frail reed, but I'm
not hard up at the moment. And you'll be getting shot
of all this falsity. It never was worth it, Maryon, ever.'

'Of course, it's lovely to be noble,' Maryon said.

'In any case, it may not happen. Adrian may have
a change of heart—or his precious Nina may drop
him.'

Maryon shook her head firmly. 'I know how actresses
tick, remember? When he's done all he can for her,
she'll drop him then. Not before.'

'So then to hell with him and all his works.'

She gave a sudden, deep sigh. 'Do you really love
me?'

'As best I can. Pretty much.'

She laid her head against him. 'Someone ought to.'

He kissed her, warmly but gently, and she snuggled closer to him. For a while they sat so, quite still, listening to the subdued ticking of the clock. At last, she rested her hand on his knee.

'No, he won't be coming now,' she said.

He placed his hand over hers. 'Shall I stay?'

'Oh yes,' she said. 'Oh yes.'

And the night grew darker still, the warm, moonless, June night, with its odours of stock and honeysuckle, and the resin of many pines. And the night creatures went their ways, the timid deer from among the snowberry, the mousing weasel, the squeaking hedge-pig, the bloody stoat and the humping badger. Moths rustled where the night-flowers bloomed, the birds of the night chirred and hooted. Along the heath the twisted pines watched the silent, blank road. And some slept, and some waked, and some were sleeping that should be waking. On a dark night of June.

2

FOUND DEAD IN CHASE

Yesterday the body of a middle-aged man was found in a remote part of Latchford Chase. The body was found in a vehicle.

Police are withholding the man's name until the relatives have been informed.

It is understood that death may been been accidental.

BODY IN CHASE

Police have still not named the man found dead in the West Brayling area of Latchford Chase on Sunday.

The body was discovered by a Forestry officer when he passed the spot on a routine patrol.

The vehicle is described as a motor-caravan and it was equipped with a gas stove. The police are said to have taken possession of a gas bottle and a length of hose.

Yesterday a police spokesman said that death may have been accidental.

MAN FOUND DEAD IN CHASE NAMED

ADRIAN STOLL IN CARAVAN TRAGEDY

Today Latchford Police named the man found dead in the West Brayling area of Latchford Chase as Adrian Stoll, the well-known film director, whose country home is at East Brayling.

Mr Stoll's body was found in a blue caravette which he often used when filming on location.

It is believed he was filming wild life in the Chase shortly before the tragedy occurred.

The discovery was made on Sunday morning by Forestry Ranger Jack Larling, who noticed an unfastened gate and went to investigate.

Police took possession of the caravette and of a gas bottle and a length of hose. A spokesman said they had not ruled out the possibility of accidental death.

Mr Stoll was expected home at the weekend. He was not known to have health or financial worries.

The police wish to hear from anyone who saw the caravette in the neighbourhood of Warren Ride on Saturday evening.

The vehicle is a dark blue Volkswagen, new model with a white elevating roof, registration number WCL 496 K.

Anyone with information should contact Latchford Police, or their local police station.

Mr Stoll, who was 55, bought East Brayling Lodge in 1965. His work as a director took him far afield, but he regarded East Brayling as his home.

Equally experienced with film and theatre, he was also admired for his work in television. He made his name with the award-winning film *The Pythoness,* based on the Goncourt prize novel by Jacques Armande. Recently he directed the musical *Chairoplanes,* which is currently playing at a West End theatre.

On Saturday he had put in a full day's work

rehearsing a play at B.B.C. Television Centre.

In 1951 Mr Stoll married the film actress, Rosalind Rix. The marriage was dissolved fourteen years later, when Miss Rix went to reside in Hollywood. She was given custody of their child, Marcus.

Mr Stoll's cousin, the novelist Edwin Keynes, also lives at East Brayling.

ADRIAN STOLL—INQUEST ADJOURNED

FOUL PLAY: 'WE HAVE TO CONSIDER IT'

The inquest into the death of film director Adrian Stoll was adjourned at Latchford Coroner's Court today, at the request of Latchford Police.

In reply to a question by the Coroner, Mr T. C. Deepdale, Latchford C.I.D. Officer Detective Inspector Herbert Metfield said that in cases of this sort foul play was always a possibility. 'We have to consider it,' he said.

He was unable to comment further at this stage, but confirmed that investigations were proceeding urgently 'here and elsewhere'.

Evidence of identification was given by the dead man's cousin, novelist and critic Edwin Keynes, of Deerview Cottage, East Brayling.

Also in court were ex-actress Maryon Britton and her daughter Jennifer, who reside at East Brayling Lodge.

Miss Britton, in a short interview, said that Stoll was expected at the Lodge last weekend. Unless he was working abroad, he usually spent his weekends at home.

Asked about his hobby of filming wild life, she said it was well known to his friends. On another occasion he had spent a night in the forest filming deer.

This time he had said nothing about his intentions, but that was quite in character. 'Adrian often did things on impulse—he was such an "alive" person.'

At B.B.C. Television Centre, a spokesman agreed that they had assisted the police with information.

The inquest has been adjourned until July 2nd.

The conference on the Stoll case was booked for 11.30 hours on June 27th. When Gently arrived at the office of the Assistant Commissioner (Crime), he found him already closeted with two men. One Gently knew: Detective Inspector Lyons, a young Met officer of reputation. The other was a fleshy-looking man in his early forties, wearing a new suit in which he seemed uncomfortable. Behind his desk, the Assistant Commissioner sat conning a typed document, with aloof disapproval. He looked up.

'Aha—Gently.'

Gently nodded. He found himself a chair. Lyons, he noticed, was looking bored: the other man was quietly sweating.

'Let's get the introductions over. Lyons, Gently, you know each other. Gently, this is Detective Inspector Metfield, who is in charge of the case at Latchford. Metfield, meet Gently. You'll learn either to love him or hate him.'

Metfield grinned nervously and reached out his hand. He had thick, jowly features and untidy dark hair.

'They still remember you at Latchford, sir,' he said. 'That job with the dope and the motorbike kids.'

'No doubt, no doubt,' the A.C. cut in sharply. 'But

we'll leave the reminiscing till later. Gently, what we need from you is your celebrated intuition, because these two gentlemen have come to an impasse. Inspector Lyons is persuaded that the crime originated in town, while Inspector Metfield is convinced that chummie is a local. And I, personally, can't decide. So now we await the wisdom of Solomon.'

Gently shrugged massively. 'Am I assigned to the case?'

'Yes,' the A.C. said. 'You most certainly are.'

'Then may I ask a fundamental question. Do we know, for a fact, that Stoll was murdered?'

The A.C. stared at Metfield. So did Lyons, coming out of his fit of ennui for a moment. The provincial Inspector goggled a bit, his fleshy mouth working, as though seeking nourishment.

'Well, the fact is,' he came out at last, 'we're not what you might call right down certain. Not one hundred per cent. It *could* have been suicide. That's why we've played it close to our chest.'

'It couldn't have been an accident?' Gently suggested.

'No, no. Oh no,' Metfield rumbled. 'No, it was a set-up job. Somebody had turned that van into a killing-bottle.'

'Perhaps you'll describe it. I've only seen the papers.'

'Well, it was like this,' Metfield said. 'There was a bottle of gas stood outside the van, and a hose leading from it to a vent in the roof. The van was locked and the windows were closed, there was just this vent in the roof open. The gas is heavier than air, of course, so it filled up the van till it spilled through the vent.'

'Where was Stoll?'

'In his sleeping-bag, sir. He'd undressed and turned in. There's a double bunk running aft, over the engine, and he'd made it up and turned in.'

'And the keys?'

'In his trouser-pocket. We had to break in when we got there.'

'No suicide note?'

'No, sir, nothing. Though there was paper in his briefcase, so he could have written one.'

Gently brooded. 'You say the windows were closed. Wouldn't that be ususual on a warm night?'

'Yes, sir—yes,' Metfield said quickly. 'I did give a bit of thought to that, sir. One of our constables owns a caravette, so I put the question to him. He reckoned that with an elevating roof, and just one man, a single vent open would be sufficient. You'd want to keep the windows closed if you could, sir, on account of the midges. They're wicked among the trees.'

'I see,' Gently said.

Metfield dabbed his brow. 'But then there's the stove to consider, sir. If it was suicide, why would he bother to bring along a hose and an extra bottle? He could just have turned on the stove, inside. That would have done the job as well. I can't see him making up the bunk and getting undressed with a hose puffing gas on him from the roof.'

'Not without a reason,' Gently said.

Metfield stared blankly. 'Well, he wouldn't, sir. And another thing. There's a spare bottle in the stowage, so if he'd wanted to play games, why not use that?'

'Did the third bottle match the other two?'

'No, sir. And I've queried the makers about it. But they could only tell me it was a recent issue in the south-east area, which includes London.'

'And no dabs, Gently,' put in the A.C. pleasantly. 'Apparently the surface of a gas bottle doesn't take them.'

'The hose?'

'It's from Woolie's,' Metfield said. 'I've got some myself, for hosing the car down.'

Gently paused, then gave a mandarin nod. 'Very well. We'll assume that Stoll was murdered. You've broken into the van and found the body. Let's hear how it goes from there.'

Metfield dabbed again. 'It's like this, sir. For one, it happened near Stoll's house. Maybe there's no direct road there, but it's only three miles off as the crow flies. Then, for two, there'd been no robbery, and there was plenty in the van to pinch—a Hasselbladt movie camera, worth over a thou, and seven hundred quid in his wallet. For three, there was the spot itself, which points to intimate local knowledge.'

'How intimate?' Gently said.

Metfield wriggled. 'I was going to explain, sir. It's a place called Mogi's Belt, after a dog that got killed there in a pheasant shoot. It's a plantation of big Scots pines, running alongside the Forestry property. But it happens to lie in the Battle Area, and Stoll should never have gone there at all. There's a wire mesh fence, six feet high, and a notice about unexploded bombs, and a gate secured with a chain and padlock—and none of it seems to have bothered Stoll.'

'It would have bothered me,' the A.C. commented. 'You can get your leg blown off in those places.'

Metfield looked sly. 'That's just my point, sir. Somehow, Stoll had got to know it was safe. Because the Army don't use it. They never have used it. It's cut off from the rest of the Area by a bog. The Forestry have tried to get permission to fell there, but you know what it's like trying to deal with the Army.'

'But then how did Stoll get in?' Gently asked.

'Easy,' Metfield said. 'Through the gate. He not only knew it was safe to go in, but he knew the padlock was broken, too. And what I'm saying is this: it called for special local knowledge, on the part of both Stoll and the chummie. Because chummie couldn't very well follow Stoll in there—he wouldn't want to turn up till several hours later.'

The A.C. delicately swung his glasses. 'Yes,' he said. 'Yes, I like it.'

'But wait a minute, sir!' Lyons broke in indignantly. 'Chummie could have got his information from the same source as Stoll. Stoll wasn't local, though he had a house there. Somebody must have told Stoll. The same person could have told chummie—or chummie might have had it from Stoll himself!'

The A.C. wagged his finger. 'Hush, Lyons. You're jumping the gun. Just now we're considering the case for Latchford. And the Inspector has only reached three.'

Metfield dabbed gratefully. 'I'm coming to it, sir. Though first I'd like to clear up another matter. We know why Stoll was where he was because we've developed the film from his camera. He'd been photographing the badgers, which have a sett there, and knowing that again needed local knowledge. The Forestry Trail pamphlet mentions the badger-gate, but it says nothing about the sett. Yet Stoll had marked its position on his copy, along with the position of the fence-gate.'

Gently stirred. 'You found that copy?'

'Yes, sir. Under the dash.'

'Have many people handled it?'

Metfield's ears coloured. 'Well, yes, sir—one or two!'

Gently sighed. 'Carry on.'

Metfield twisted his damp handkerchief. 'For four, sir! Stoll was carrying his will with him, in his brief-case.'

'His will!'

'Yes sir, his will.'

The A.C. beamed happily at Gently. 'You've set the Chief Super's ears up,' he said to Metfield. 'I was sure you'd get a reaction, with that.'

Metfield looked embarrassedly pleased: he studied the handkerchief.

'What sort of a will?' Gently almost snapped.

'Well, a proper will, sir,' Metfield said, apologetically. 'It was got out by his lawyers up here in town.'

'A recent will?'

'No, sir, not recent. It was dated October '65. That was soon after his divorce went through. He'd needed to have made a new will then.'

'So,' Gently said. 'Now let's have it.'

Metfield took a fresh grip on his rag. 'The house and a big slice of the money goes to the co-respondent, Maryon Britton. She's the woman who's been living with him at the Lodge, her and her daughter, Jennifer. On an estimate, the property is worth forty thousand, and the contents may be worth more. Then she gets thirty thousand cash for certain, or one-third of Stoll's investments, whichever is greater.'

'Quite a carrot,' murmured the A.C.

'Yes, sir,' Metfield said. 'Then there's her daughter, she's down for five thousand when she comes of age, at twenty-one. And Stoll's cousin, who lives down there. He gets Stoll's cars, plus two thousand. The flat at Campden Hill and the balance of the estate go into trust for Stoll's son in America. We're trying to contact the son now. The U.S. Embassy is locating him for us.'

'Are the cars anything special?' the A.C. queried.

'There's the caravette, sir, and a new Bentley.'

'The devil there is!' The A.C. was a Bentley man. 'That's enough to do murder for, for a start.'

'Yes, sir,' Metfield agreed modestly. 'It does add up to a fair old lump. And since we know now that Stoll was going to change his will, it adds up to a fair old motive, as well.' He glanced at Gently, still apologetic. 'We've got that from his lawyers, sir,' he said. 'Stoll made an appointment with them last week, when he collected the old will from them.'

'We can also guess why, Gently,' the A.C. said. 'But every dog in its own kennel. Let's have the picture at Brayling, Metfield. It seems to have collusion written all over it.'

Metfield licked his lips—or rather, performed an action that gave the impression that he was swallowing his tongue. 'The fact is,' he said, his eyes rounding, 'that the cousin is sleeping with Stoll's woman. His name is Keynes, Edwin Keynes, and he writes books or some caper. He lives in a cottage in the village and doesn't have two halfpennies to rub together. Well, of course, I wanted alibis, and Keynes and the woman didn't want to give one. But in the end, I got them to admit that he spent Saturday night at the Lodge. Then the daughter agreed that he was there, too, and they could both of them speak for the daughter—a mutual alibi of the interested persons. Meaning sweet Fanny Adams.'

'There was transport available?' The A.C. led him.

'Plenty of transport,' Metfield said. 'Maryon Britton drives a Sunbeam Rapier, Keynes has got a Hillman Imp. And listen to this: I found three more gas bottles, two at the Lodge and one at the cottage. They claim they bought them in Feb. of last year, when we were having the strike and the blackouts.'

'Did you check that?' Gently cut in.

'Well, yes, I took it up,' Metfield conceded. 'The bottles were issued about when they said. But it does prove one thing—they knew about gas bottles.'

'Have you checked for recent purchases?' Gently said.

'Yes,' Metfield said, his ears reddening. 'Only they could have bought the bottle anywhere in the southeast, and I've been able to check only in my district.'

'They know about gas bottles,' the A.C. said smoothly. 'That's what will appeal to the Public Prosecutor.

Nice if we could pin them down, I agree. But I'm sure a jury will take the point.'

Gently grunted. 'I've heard nothing yet to suggest it will get as far as a jury.'

'Circumstantial, certainly,' the A.C. said. 'But there's more to come. Keep bowling, Metfield.'

'Yes, sir.' Metfield dabbed a little. 'So I've made a few inquiries in the village. Keynes has got a young-ster staying with him, a kid called Turner, who's try-ing to make a living as a painter. He's got no money, neither has Keynes. I reckon the pair of them were living off Maryon Britton. And she and her daugh-ter were living off Stoll, so Stoll was supporting the whole bunch.' Metfield did the trick with his tongue again. 'Now suppose Stoll's decided he'd had enough. Suppose he decides to pull the rug out—change his will—set up with a fresh woman. Along with the rest, and a notion about gas bottles, I'd say it was adding up to a case.'

Gently stared. 'Can we prove that about Stoll?'

'Yes, sir, I think so. Enough, anyway.'

'This is where Lyons comes in,' the A.C. said. 'Though not, I'm afraid, with compulsive enthusiasm. Briefly, Inspector.'

Lyons looked up languidly: he had been distaste-fully eyeing his trousers. 'Without prejudice,' he said, 'and without comment. Stoll had been running after Nina Walling.'

'Nina Walling—the actress?'

Lyons nodded his head, once. 'For what it's worth. She's currently playing the lead in Stoll's musical, at the Capri. Dark, rakish and trendy. The gossip says she was playing him along. Stoll could have made her a star, of course. She was busy sleeping her way to the top.'

'I see,' Gently said. 'Have you talked to her?'

Lyons ghosted a shrug. 'It cost the Special Fund.

She isn't shattered. Still without prejudice, her father is Oscar Walling, described as a financier.'

His eyes held Gently's for a moment, quizzically: but the name meant nothing to Gently.

The A.C. gave his glasses a swing. 'So that's the case for Latchford, Gently,' he said. 'Proximity, local knowledge needed, three people with a critical financial interest. Gaps, of course. We need to show that these three people knew of the will, knew of Nina and Stoll's probable intentions, knew where to find him on Saturday night. But those are mere routine questions. I'm sure you can soon fill in the answers. The case has merit. No doubt your intuition is already beginning to twitch.'

Gently steepled his fingers. 'But there's an alternative case?'

'Oh yes. And equally attractive.'

'So, without prejudice, I'll suspend my intuition.'

' "I knew it would be your answer",' the A.C. said, in heavy quotes.

Blondie, the much-fancied policewoman, fetched in coffee on a tray—not the canteen stuff, but regular ground coffee, bubbling out its soul in a silver-plated percolator. The A.C. was mother. Since his renouncement of nicotine, he had become an enthusiastic connoisseur of coffee. He drank it black and well steeped in Demarara, silently, with a glint in his eye. Lyons also drank it black: Gently with a drip of cream. Metfield instantly lost caste by plopping in cream in moronic dollops. The A.C. eyed him with a curious expression, like a don who perceives a false quantity in Latin.

The ritual ended.

'Good,' the A.C. said. 'Now we'll hear Lyons with full prejudice.'

Lyons placed his cup fastidiously on the tray, sat

back, and elegantly crossed his legs. He paused for a moment, admiring the legs.

'Perhaps I'd best put it this way,' he said. 'Somebody has lately conned Stoll out of fifty thousand pounds. And Stoll received confirmation on Thursday of last week.'

He paused again.

'Who conned him?' Gently said.

'The father of his current mistress, Nina Walling.'

'This Oscar Walling?'

Lyons nodded. 'Who financed Stoll's musical at the Capri. Or appeared to finance it. Because what seems really to have happened is that Stoll involuntarily backed his own show, while supposing his money was adroitly invested in a package tour money-spinner, Torotours.'

'And Stoll found out about it?'

'On Thursday.' Lyons indicated the sheet on the A.C.'s desk. 'That's a report from the private investigation firm, Sekurit, which we found in Stoll's flat. Apparently Stoll invested in Torotours without seeking professional advice. When it came to the notice of his solicitors, Branch and Parkway, they advised him to have Torotours checked out. On his instructions, they employed Sekurit, and the report was delivered to him on Thursday. On Thursday he knew that Torotours was a swindle, and that Walling had taken him for a ride.'

'And the money had really gone into Stoll's musical?'

Lyons smiled a thin-lipped smile. 'Well, it certainly didn't go into Torotours, and Walling supplied the backing for *Chairoplanes*. Of course, if *Chairoplanes* had been a hit it would probably have worked out for Walling. But it hasn't been a hit. It's coming off next week. So Stoll's fifty thou has gone down the drain. Which doubtless left Walling with only a bright smile to offer when Stoll beat on his door, threatening fire and slaughter.'

The A.C. gave his glasses an impatient flip. 'Let me fill in the background, Gently,' he said. 'The Fraud Squad is poised to move in on Torotours, and so are Her Majesty's Servants. Torotours was a neat scheme to swindle both the public and the Inland Revenue—two birds with one stone.' He beamed benignly: the A.C. had a weakness for ingenious frauds. 'It worked like this. Walling set up an agency that offered luxury Spanish holidays at moderate prices. For the first year, which was last year, he was offering an honest deal. This gained Torotours a reputation and heavy bookings for the present season, but when this year's customers arrived in Spain they found rather a different picture. Their luxury accommodation was not available—the fault of the Spanish agents, of course!—and they were given alternative accommodation in fifth-rate hotels. If they complained, they were issued with credit vouchers, valid when they re-booked with Toro-tours; and if they still complained, they were referred to some suitably small print on their booking-form. Legally, they didn't have a leg to stand on, as a few who tried it soon discovered.'

The A.C. reached for a scribbling pad and quickly jotted down figures.

'Torotours had bookings for four thousand units at £125 per unit. Cost of travel and low-standard accommodation estimated at £50. Leaving a gross profit of £300,000, subject to a cut for the Spanish agents.' He threw down his ball pen. 'Substantial, wasn't it? Or would have been, except for mass cancellations.'

Gently looked owlish. 'But if it was legal?'

'Aha.' The A.C. activated his glasses. 'Walling was greedy. He tried his pranks on the Inland Revenue as well. His Spanish agents sent him fictitious invoices

for the luxury accommodation, and he tried to work
them off on his taxman, who was a little astuter than
he was. So we were alerted, and the Spanish police.
And now the Fraud Squad has the evidence. That
low-standard accommodation, an alleged emergency,
was booked as far back as last November. *Entre nous,*
I've o.k.'d a warrant. We'll be raiding Torotours today.'

Gently looked more owlish. 'And Stoll invested in
this racket?'

'Walling was a pal of his,' Lyons said quickly.
'They'd had a number of show business deals together.
Walling's flat is only two doors from Stoll's.'

'And don't forget the daughter,' the A.C. added.
'That circumstance would probably cloud Stoll's
judgement. Also, Torotours began as a bona fide
project—perhaps still was, when Stoll invested.'

'So what's the theory?'

Lyons leaned forward eagerly. 'Walling couldn't
raise fifty thou to repay Stoll. And he knew that if
Stoll showed us the Sekurit report it would mean a
twicer at the very least. So what was he to do?'

Gently hunched. 'He might have asked for time to
pay. Presumably Walling isn't entirely broke, and an
offer of a few thou might have saved him.'

'But suppose Stoll wouldn't agree?'

'Then there'd still be Nina Walling. Stoll wouldn't
want to send her father to prison.'

Lyons made derisive throat noises. 'You haven't met
Nina Walling! If Daddy stood in her way, I wouldn't
fancy his chances.'

Gently sighed softly. 'Very well, then. We'll accept
the hypothesis that Walling was desperate. We'll suppose that every other avenue was closed to him, and
that only Stoll's demise could solve his problem. Has
Walling a record of violence?'

'Well . . . no!'

'Does he mix with people who have?'

'No—well, not exactly! But I'll bet he knows a few who could put him on to a rough boy, if he needed one.'

'Do hold your horses, Gently,' the A.C. said reprovingly. 'Lyons does have a case worth consideration. For example, Walling was away from town last weekend. And the weekend before that he was staying at the Lodge.'

'And he doesn't have an alibi!' Lyons snapped. 'At least, he hasn't come up with one yet. And he knows all about Stoll's hobby of filming wild life—actually made a trip with him, to the New Forest.'

'So, one way or another,' the A.C. soothed, 'Walling is at least as suspect as the others. No knowledge of wills is necessary in his case, and he may have known in advance where Stoll was going. Stoll could have planned his badger trip the previous weekend, and Walling may even have explored the ground with him.'

'Though it would still need special local knowledge,' Metfield broke in anxiously.

'Yes,' the A.C. agreed kindly. 'It would still need that.'

Lyons recrossed his legs with a quick, irritable movement. 'I don't see it matters that Walling doesn't have form. There are professional killers and there are oncers. Nobody's claiming that Walling's a pro. This isn't a pro-type killing, in any case. It's about as amateur as they come. Just the sort of thing a oncer would pull if he didn't know about violence, and didn't want to.'

'And that's Walling's type?' Gently asked.

'That's precisely Walling's type.'

'I understand he's a homosexual,' the A.C. said brightly. 'The plump sort. A de Charlus.'

Lyons sniffed. 'He lives with a boy friend, a youngster he passes off as his secretary. It's a big flat. They have half of it, his daughter occupies the rest. I've talked to all three of them, keeping it casual. The kid and Nina were there over the weekend. Walling wasn't. He says he was in Brighton, but he was evasive when I tried to probe. He left after breakfast, according to his friend, and wasn't back till late on Sunday. Nina played her two houses on Saturday and got in around midnight. The kid waited up for her. Walling took his car, a Jaguar 420, and a weekend case.'

'Any purchase of gas bottles?'

'No,' Lyons said sulkily. 'But you can buy them all over London.'

'Any sightings of Walling in the Latchford area?'

'If there were,' Lyons said, 'he'd be inside now.'

'In fact, another circumstantial case?'

'All right,' Lyons said savagely. 'This is circumstantial too. But it's asking a lot fewer questions than the case at the other end, and the questions it does ask we can get the answers to. Walling had a clear, strong, urgent motive, plus knowledge and adequate opportunity.'

'Though he did have alternative courses open to him,' Metfield rumbled.

Lyons shut his mouth tight and glared at nowhere.

'Well, well,' the A.C. purred contentedly. He sat back in his chair with a pleased smile. 'I think that concludes the evidence, Gently,' he said. 'So now I'll call on your contribution. On the one hand we have this faded ex-actress, with a fortune about to slip from her grasp, and on the other a homosexual financier, with a prison sentence staring him in the face. Greed and ruin, a nice balance. I must confess I look forward to your opinion.'

Gently slid his pipe from his pocket and began polishing the bowl against his palm. Then he blew through it once or twice. 'How much do we know about Stoll?' he asked.

'What about Stoll?'

'About his character. About whether it was stable or unstable.'

The A.C. flicked a quick look at Lyons.

'He wasn't a mixer, sir,' Metfield said. 'He'd had that place at Brayling for a few years, but he never made friends with the folk round there.'

'Which means damn-all,' Lyons said. 'Why would he mix with a lot of swede-bashers? No doubt he'd have temperament, doing his job, but I haven't heard he was round the twist.'

'But a noticeable temperament?' Gently asked.

'Well, about what you'd expect,' Lyons said. 'I hear he was tough with actors and scriptwriters, but that's what directors are paid to be.'

'Rather a lonely man.'

'Perhaps he was.'

'His wife, his child, long gone. His mistress taken up with another man. A scheming young actress stringing him along. Then his show coming off next week. And the discovery that a friend had swindled him. It all seems to have been building up, rather. Not a great deal left in it for Stoll.'

The A.C.'s glasses switched a full circle. 'Carry on,' he said. 'This is vintage.'

Gently grunted. 'We don't like suicide, because the extra gas bottle is an elaboration. But suppose that was in Stoll's mind. Suppose this was his last, his most subtle production. He is leaving us a picture of normal behaviour, of a man in eager pursuit of his hobby: with the hose and the extra bottle, why should we dream he was committing suicide? So we search the van and find the will, which directs suspicion to Maryon Britton—and sends us hotfoot to Stoll's lawyers, who bring Walling to our attention. By the purchase of an extra gas bottle and a few yards of Woolworth's hose, Stoll has succeeded in stage-managing the very conference that has just taken place in this office.'

'You devil!' the A.C. exclaimed.

'In fact, we are Stoll's dupes,' Gently said. 'We are playing his script for him. This is act one curtain. Next, we have to put the transgressors through hell.'

'No!' the A.C. exclaimed. 'Enough, Gently!'

'I admit, it's circumstantial,' Gently said. 'But it fits as well as the other two theories, and it would save a packet of taxpayers' money.'

The A.C. thumped his desk. 'I said enough!'

'That's my provisional opinion,' Gently said.

The A.C. put on his glasses, adjusted them, and treated Gently to a grade one stare.

'All right,' he said, 'all right, Gently. Message received and understood. So we don't know enough to start wildcat theories and to call in our oracle to adjudicate. But our oracle has been called in, and our oracle will duly apply himself. I want this little lot sorted out, preferably before the Sunday papers can get their hands on it. Is that clear?'

'Clear,' Gently said.

The A.C. gave him another stare. Lyons was examining his trousers. Metfield, pop-eyed, was blushing, aware of sudden thunder.

3

The A.C. dismissed them, and switched his attention to a working lunch with a Cabinet Minister. Gently entertained his mice, town and country, in the canteen: the executive end.

Metfield, by now, was completely confused. His so-certain case seemed to have gone through the window. He sat silently masticating his New Scotland Yard viands, his flush continual and his gaze vacant.

Lyons, too, was far from chatty. He was a pale-complexioned young man with thin lips and precise sideburns. He was being tipped in Met quarters as a likely recruit for the Central Office—Gently rather hoped not; Lyons seemed to lack humour.

So the meal was on the quiet side, with no mention of the Stoll affair. Gently, as he had intended, had returned the case to square one. No more theories. The next step was to go digging. At this end, naturally; because this end was nearest to hand.

After lunch, he dismissed Metfield to pursue his bucolic inquiries at Latchford, and himself, with Lyons and a driver, battled through the traffic to Campden Hill.

The two flats, Stoll's and Walling's, were in Dorchester Road, at a polite distance from Kensington Church Street. It was a road of late Regency plaster-front terraces, still impressive, though London-seedy.

The architects, alack, had known nothing of cars, or of their dire need to come to rest: along each broad pavement stretched a tightly-packed column, as yet unembarrassed by yellow lines. They were the usual democratic metropolitan sample, dusty Rolls by rusty Citroën, and exhibited the familiar aspect of being parked for ever, with half that period unexpired. Behind them the villas looked out sullenly, even though enlivened by fresh paint. A few scaling planes, with town-dusty foliage, sprouted irregularly from either pavement.

Gently's driver cruised ever more slowly between the breechless ranks of abandoned cars, but in the end had to double-park—it was clearly the way of life, in Dorchester Road.

'Shall we look over Stoll's flat first, sir?' Lyons asked.

Gently shook his head and indicated Walling's. A pale ghost behind the net curtains had been watching the policemen alight below. Gently mounted some tiled steps and applied his thumb to an elaborate brass bell-push. Chimes sounded sleepily within. The door opened to reveal a slender young man.

'Police. Is Mr. Walling at home?'

The young man stared with unwinking, large eyes. He was dressed in faded skinfit jeans and a wine-coloured shirt, open down to the midriff. He had dark, shoulder-length hair and fine-boned features, with a small mouth and chin.

'I don't know. He may be,' he said quickly.

'What's your name?' Gently asked.

The young man's stare was quite expressionless. 'I'm Messiter,' he said. 'Mr Walling's secretary.'

'And you think he might be in?'

'I don't know. He may be.'

'So you said before,' Gently said. 'Like that, we'll just have to take a chance.'

He pushed in across the threshold, making Messiter

give ground. The young man backed off agilely, then halted, in a cluttered hall.

'Very well,' he said. 'I'll try to find him. Perhaps you'll just wait here.'

'Thank you,' Gently said. 'Please don't be long.'

Messiter ducked through a curtain at the end of the hall.

Lyons closed the street door, and they waited. There was no sound from behind the curtain. A faint smell of incense hung about the hall, which was lit only by a fanlight over the street door. The walls were muffled with floral tapestry, and vases and knick-knacks stood about on stands. A bundle of Polynesian spears, very ancient and dusty, were stuffed into an umbrella-stand near the door. An odd, over-filled place: somehow devoid of effective character.

The curtain twitched again: a man appeared; he came hesitatingly towards them. He was aged about fifty, of plump build, with a short neck and bowed shoulders. He was wearing a green silk smock and loose trousers that suggested a judo kit, and embroidered slippers. He had fluffy, greying hair, and his large features were netted with wrinkles, like crumpled brown paper.

'Oscar Walling?' Gently said.

'Yes—yes!' The man was smiling ingratiatingly. He had a reedy but cultivated voice and appealing pale blue eyes.

'I'm Detective Chief Superintendent Gently. I'm investigating the death of Adrian Stoll.'

'Yes—yes—poor Adrian! Yes, of course. I understand.'

He made a quick, dipping motion forward, and threw open a door to Gently's left. Then he stood smiling and motioning them through, with soft white hands, on which rings glinted.

They entered a large, lofty room, with the same

appearance of clutter as the hall outside. In the centre
stood a huge, overstuffed sofa, piled with tasselled
cushions and books. A rosewood desk occupied one
wall, and fitted bookcases two others; several outsize
chairs, echoing the sofa, were disposed to monopolize
the remaining floor-space. Then there was an infilling
of stands and whatnots, bearing vases, figures and
native carvings; and everywhere books, papers, peri-
odicals and piles of sheet music. Two standard lamps,
with vast shades, presided over the collection. In the
bay window stood a music-stand; a violin lay on a
chair beside it.

Walling bobbed in after them and closed the door,
which was heavy and lined with draught-excluder.
He waved them to seats. Lyons ignored him. Gently
perched on an arm of the giant sofa. Walling hesitated,
smiling, then emptied a chair, and plumped down
in it, his short legs dangling. He looked hopefully at
Gently.

'Yes—poor Adrian! Yes—I wish I could be of some
help to you! But I've spoken to this other gentleman already. There is really nothing I can add.'

'That's unfortunate,' Gently said. 'Have you been
to your office today?'

'M-my office?'

'Torotours. 221B Hapsburgh Place.'

'Torotours?' Walling gazed at Gently, his smile
flickering on and off. 'Yes—yes—that's my company—
Torotours, in Hapsburgh Place.'

'So have you been there today?'

'Well—no—not today. I'm not personally engaged in
running it, you know. I have a good manager—very
good man.'

'I think you should ring him,' Gently said.

'What—why?' Walling's eyes were dithering. 'Why
should I ring him?'

'I think you should. Then we can get on with our little chat.'

Walling sat uncertainly for a moment, the smile leaking from his crumpled face; then he darted up, crossed to the desk, and dialled a number with a silver pencil.

'Stella—hallo? Get me Parsons, darling.' He shored his plump bottom on the desk. 'Hullo? What? I want Parsons! You're not Parsons. What? Who——?'

Slowly, the instrument sank from his ear and was dropped back unsteadily on its rest. He turned his face away from the policemen.

'Dear God. Oh dear God.'

Gently was watching him. 'Will that help your memory?'

Walling shook his fluffy head. His bowed shoulders were more deeply bowed; he looked like an old lady who had taken a cowardly blow in the wind.

'But he said . . . he swore he would give me a chance!'

'How long did you have to find the money?'

'A week. He swore he wouldn't . . .'

'On Thursday, was that?'

Walling hugged himself, groaning.

Gently pulled the Sekurit report from his pocket. 'Then of course, you've seen this before?'

Walling turned, fearfully; he flinched. His seamed features looked blurred, ill.

'B-but we were friends!' he stammered. 'Friends. I'd always found him backing . . . always. I used to stay with him, travel with him—he was the closest friend I had! And there was Nina . . . he loved Nina. How could he do this thing to me?'

'You took his money,' Gently said.

Walling's hands waved anguishedly. 'But that was just figures! I'm a man of figures—making figures work for people is my business. I had to make the figures right for his musical—that was Nina's big chance, too. And who was taking the risk? It wasn't Adrian! I had still to produce figures for him, based on Torotours.'

'All the same, you were deceiving him.'

'Couldn't he have trusted me?'

'Not after *Chairoplanes* flopped, I imagine. Then all you had going for you was Torotours, and this report showed him what that was worth.'

'But if he'd just kept calm! I could have made it come right.'

Gently shook his head. 'Torotours was doomed.'

'No, I could have sacked the manager and put things right—if only he hadn't shown you that meddlesome report!'

Gently fanned himself with the report. 'He didn't,' he said.

Walling's pale eyes jumped. 'He didn't?'

'No. We found this in his flat. Stoll kept his word. He didn't shop you.'

'B-but——!' Walling jerked off the desk and stood staring at Gently, his eyes wild. Then, with a moan, he dropped into the desk-chair. He covered his face.

'I want my lawyer,' he said.

A knock sounded at the door, and Messiter entered. His unwavering eyes took in the scene. He crossed silently to the desk and straightened the telephone, which Walling had replaced askew. He stood before Walling.

'Did you call me, sir?'

Walling's hands dropped from his face. He was trembling. He stared up at Messiter with a haggard, unfocusing expression.

'No—no. I didn't call.'

'I wondered if you wished me to telephone.'

Walling shook his head.

'I was about to bring you a drink, sir. Perhaps you would like me to fetch it now.'

Walling said nothing; Gently said nothing. Messiter left and returned with a brandy. He stood by obstinately while Walling sipped it, then collected the glass and retired. Walling looked less grey now. He had ceased to tremble, and his eyes had lost their muzziness.

'That was a trick, Superintendent,' he said, thickly. 'You trapped me into making those admissions.'

Gently shrugged. 'Nothing I can't prove. And it saved us time at the outset.'

'I needn't have admitted all that about Adrian.'

'You would have to have done, sooner or later. Stoll didn't commission Sekurit for kicks. Once he'd seen this report, he'd have been after you.'

'But you couldn't *prove* that!'

'Didn't he show you the report?'

'He . . . I . . . !' Walling faltered wretchedly.

'So your dabs are on it,' Gently lied. 'Why do you have to make us work for it?'

Walling ran fingers through his wool-like hair. 'Please,' he said. 'I didn't kill him. All the rest, I admit that. But I didn't kill him. Please believe me!'

'Then what were you going to do?' Gently said.

'I was going to pay him back his money.'

'The whole fifty thousand?'

'Yes—yes! Though perhaps not all of it, not within a week.'

'Within how long?'

'I don't know!' Walling moaned. 'It's a matter of figures, it takes time. But a percentage, yes, I would have found him that, and Adrian wouldn't have gone back on me.'

'Didn't he mean a week when he said a week?'

'Yes—of course—but he was angry.'

'You thought you could get round him.'

'Yes—a percentage! Believe me, it would have been all right.'

Gently slowly shook his head. 'No,' he said. 'It wouldn't have been all right. Stoll wanted his money, not a percentage, not a Houdini stunt with figures. You could trust him, maybe, to sit on the report till the time limit was up, but after that he was going to act, and there was only one way to stop him.'

'Please, no!' Walling wailed. 'How can you say that, when you didn't know him?'

Gently grunted. 'You knew him. And you were ready to believe he'd broken his word.'

'But you tricked me into it!'

'You still believed it. Stoll's word wasn't to be trusted. And you couldn't find the money anyway. So how else was the plot going to end?'

Walling raked at his hair again. His wrinkled face looked clownishly woebegone. His short legs hung down pathetically, the feet barely touching the carpet. He gulped a breath.

'How could it have been me, when I was at Brighton the whole weekend?'

'At Brighton?'

Walling winced, and threw an apprehensive look towards the door.

'I drove down after breakfast on Saturday. I didn't arrive back till late on Sunday. Please, that's the truth—Nigel can verify the times.'

'Didn't he go with you?'

'No—no. This was a little trip on my own. Adrian had upset me very much, you know, and I wanted a quiet weekend to soothe me down.'

'I see,' Gently said. 'All on your own. And of course, you can tell us where you stayed.'

Walling cast another look at the door. 'Yes,' he said. 'Yes. It's just a little place I know.'

'Then suppose you let us know it, too.'

'Well, it's a small place—very small.'

'Too small to have an address?'

'No—no!' Walling swallowed. 'It's just—private. That's all!'

He stared appealingly at Gently, who returned the stare stonily. Hastily Walling grabbed a pad and ball-pen from the desk and scribbled something down. He tore off the sheet and handed it to Gently. It read:

'Vivian Chance, Flat 3, Kyles Court.

PLEASE don't mention in front of NIGEL ! ! !'

Silently, Gently passed the sheet to Lyons, who glanced at it, then tucked it away in his wallet. Walling watched them eagerly, his pale eyes pleading.

'So you are known at this—small place?' Gently said.

'Yes—yes. You've only to ask.'

'You met several people who could identify you?'

Walling's hand fluttered. 'Well . . . the one.'

"Just . . . the *one*?'

'I-I didn't go out much! I went down to soothe my nerves, you know. To relax. The sea air. This p-place has a marine view.'

'And you think we're going to swallow that?'

'But please—it's true! Nigel will tell you when I was away. And you can inquire at the—the hotel. Please! The m-m-manager will give his word!'

Lyons said casually: 'I think it stinks.'

'Oh, dear God!' Walling wailed.

'I don't think the manager's word is going to help much,' Gently said. 'The way you are placed, it will take more than that. Somebody followed Stoll out to the forest. Somebody put him to sleep for good. Somebody with a very strong reason. And we have one man's word that you were in Brighton.'

'It isn't going to stand up,' Lyons drawled.

'It certainly won't convince a jury,' Gently said. 'I don't know what the Fraud Squad have in mind for you, but I think they're probably wasting their time.'

Walling dragged agonizedly on his hair. 'No!' he cried, his reedy voice hitting sudden falsetto. 'You can't believe that—it's too completely incredible! I would never have dreamed of killing Adrian.'

'Then who would?' Lyons asked boredly.

'Who—who? There's Maryon Britton! She had reason enough, hadn't she? And she was on the spot, too.'

Gently gazed at him. '*Did* she have reason?'

'Yes. Yes! He was going to ditch her. And he was going to change his will, cut her out. None of that crowd was getting a penny!'

'And *you* knew that?'

Walling faltered. 'Yes. Yes. Yes, I knew it.'

'How, Mr Walling?'

Walling swallowed. 'I was there when they had the row.'

Gently gazed at him a while longer, then began deliberately filling his pipe. Walling was trembling again; there was a tremble or tic at the corner of his mouth. Gently lit the pipe and looked round for an ashtray. Walling bobbed to his feet and fetched one. His eyes avoided Gently's. He plumped down again: his mouth was still twitching.

Gently puffed. 'When?'

Walling looked sulky. 'The weekend before last.'

'When you went down with Stoll?'

Walling nodded. 'We were old friends. He often invited me.'

'What happened?'

'This row blew up. Adrian saw Keynes kissing Maryon. Not that there was anything special about that, because Adrian had known about it for a long time. But perhaps he hadn't actually seen them kissing before—or perhaps he just wanted an occasion for the row.'

'Was it a violent row?'

'There was plenty said. It didn't come to physical violence. They knew all about my daughter, of course, and that made splendid ammunition. Adrian didn't show up very well, though naturally he held the whip-hand. I was horribly infra dig. They practically accused me of pimping my own daughter.'

'Did Stoll tell Miss Britton she would have to get out?'

'That was the message,' Walling nodded. 'Also he hinted about the will. Said he would have to revise his previous dispositions.'

'The will was specifically referred to?'

'Yes—yes! Though he didn't actually say what he was going to do.'

'What did he say, then?'

'Well, he wanted them to sweat on it, so he said he would let them know the details when he'd talked to his lawyer.'

'About the will?'

'Yes, about the will. And about when Maryon would have to get out. Because there was no doubt about that, you know. Maryon and Jennifer were getting the boot.'

Gently puffed once or twice. 'And after the row?'

Walling made a furtive snatch at his locks. 'After the row we left for town. There was nothing to stay for, after that.'

'You travelled with Stoll?'

'Yes. Yes.'

'Did he refer to what had taken place?'

'No, he didn't. He didn't talk at all. He was in one of his brooding fits.'

'He didn't discuss other matters? Like filming wild life.'

'No. He scarcely said a word.'

'Before the row, did he talk about that?'

Walling shook his head. 'No. Nothing at all.'

'So you, of course, wouldn't have known his pro-
gramme?'

Walling stared. 'How should I?'

'Being such an old friend,' Gently said. 'Often invited down to Brayling. Surely you'd have given Stoll
a hand with his hobby?'

Walling's eyes widened. 'B-but no, I never did!
Adrian rarely took anyone filming with him. It was
something he did quite on his own—all we knew about
it was the film show, afterwards.'

'Have you never been in the Chase with him?'

'No—scarcely ever! A picnic once, two years ago.'

'At the Warren Ride site?'

Walling shook his head, stupidly.

'Near Mogi's Belt?'

Walling's head continued shaking.

'Still, you've had plenty of opportunity,' Gently
said. 'You could have familiarized yourself with the
forest. You could have discovered the attraction of
Mogi's Belt. It could have been you who sent Stoll
there.'

Walling wailed and grappled with his hair.

'We have only your word that you didn't,' Gently
said.

'It sounds like a case to me, sir,' Lyons said blandly.
'Especially with this package tour swindle in the background.'

Gently puffed. 'Well?' he asked.

Walling got up from his chair. He was shaking. 'I
want my lawyer!' he quavered. 'I'm not saying any
more. You haven't been fair. I want my lawyer.'

'He can't alter the facts,' Gently said.

'I want him,' Walling said weakly. 'I want him!'

Gently considered the financier through an issue of
smoke. 'Very well, then,' he said. 'That will do for
now.'

'That will d-do . . . ?'

'For now,' Gently said. 'Which doesn't mean we shan't be back later.' He trailed another thoughtful ribbon of smoke. 'Send in Messiter, will you?'

Walling gaped, and his eyes rolled. For a moment it seemed he was going to speak; then his twitching mouth closed, and he wobbled unsteadily to the door.

Messiter answered questions flatly, standing before Gently with quiet poise. Walling had departed on Saturday at ten-thirty a.m. and returned at nine p.m. on Sunday. Messiter had packed him a weekend bag. Walling had stated he was visiting a relative; he had a married sister living in Hove with whom he occasionally spent a weekend. Messiter recalled no visit from Stoll on Thursday, but added that he was absent during the afternoon.

'And where did you spend your weekend?' Gently asked.

Messiter didn't flicker an eyelid. 'After Mr Walling left I tidied the flat, then I went up town to do some shopping. I had lunch at the Isola Bella, in Frith Street. In the afternoon I visited the Museum. I returned here to have my tea, and in the evening I practised a violin part. When Miss Nina came in from the theatre I made her a light supper. On Sunday I visited friends at Hampstead, walked on the Heath, then played music with them.'

'You remember it very well,' Gently said.

Messiter accepted the compliment without comment.

'How much did you see of Stoll?'

'Mr Stoll was a frequent visitor.'

'But what sort of terms were you on?'

'Mr Stoll was a close friend of Mr Walling's.'

'Didn't he ever talk to you about his hobby?'

'I had few conversations with Mr Stoll.'

It was stony ground: Gently gave up, and they left
the overcrowded, aromatic flat. Lyons produced the
keys of Stoll's flat and let them in through a gilt-
ornamented door. Inside, he turned eagerly to Gently.

'What do you think, sir?' he asked.

'I think you'd better check Walling's alibi, and leave
him to the Fraud Squad for the moment.'

Lyons's face fell. 'I'd like to pull him in, sir.'

'Then you'll be pulling in his lawyer as well. Check
the alibi. Walling isn't going to run. If the alibi is
punk you'll have something to hit him with.'

'Sir, I'll take a chance that he's chummie.'

Gently shrugged and pushed past him into the flat.

It was a smaller flat than Walling's, but it contained
one considerable room. By contrast it was sparsely
furnished, mostly with expensive reproduction pieces.
The suite in the large lounge was Adams. The chairs
tended to be grouped at one end. Immediately one got
the impression of a projection room, and the projector
was there, in a mock-period cabinet. In place of Walling's litter of sheet-music and books was a tidier litter
of duplicated scripts. They were strewn on the carpet
around the Adams sofa, on which one lay open, its
face to the cushions. Lyons picked it up.

'"The Romantic Painters",' he read. '"5. Parkes
Bonington. By Ivan Webster." That's what Stoll was
working on, sir, on Saturday. It's a new TV series for
the autumn.'

'Then he must have called in here after he left
Television Centre.'

'Yes, sir. He had his Bentley at the Centre. He'd
have come back here to pick up the van. He rents two
garages in the mews.'

Gently took the script. It was cut and annotated in
slashing red pencil. The notes were scribbled in a
semi-legible hand that combined flaring capitals with
inchoate minuscules. 'No! No! ! !' 'Cut to 76! ! !' 'All

ref. to S. OUT!!!' At first sight it seemed virtually impossible to pick up what thread of the script was left. Gently dropped it back on the sofa.

'Did Stoll mention his plans to anyone at the Centre?'

'Nobody I've spoken to,' Lyons said. 'You get the impression that Stoll wasn't a chatterer.'

'Comment on his manner?'

'Nothing useful. He blew his top on two occasions. But that was how he used to work, how most directors carry on.'

'When did he leave?'

'Six-thirty.'

'He would have to have eaten somewhere.'

'Out,' Lyons said. 'He didn't eat here. His daily woman found it tidy.'

'Try to trace the restaurant,' Gently said. 'His contacts that evening are top priority. Anyone Stoll may have dropped a word to. We must know how chummie tracked him out there.' He brooded. 'Allow an hour for the meal. Then he dropped off the script and perhaps collected some gear. That would make it around eight when he set out. Which means he reached Latchford at about ten.'

'When it was getting dark, sir.'

Gently nodded. 'Probably quite dark, when he got to the forest. Meaning any picnickers or visitors had left, and not a soul around to see. Like Metfield, I think Stoll wasn't followed in there, because following lights would be too conspicuous. So chummie had to *know* where Stoll was heading—and if Walling is chummie, we'll have to show how he knew.'

'Understood, sir,' Lyons said bleakly.

'And that's just a beginning,' Gently said. 'Because unless we can also show him buying a bottle of gas, there'll be little bonus in setting up Walling.'

Lyons chewed his lip disconsolately: this really

did sound like the thumbs down! But then his attention was attracted by a Volvo which was trying to park
at the kerb outside.

'Sir—that's Nina Walling!'

Gently turned to regard the Volvo. It was being
manoeuvred by a dark-haired young woman with
pale, dolly-bird features.

'Ask her to step in.'

'Yes, sir!'

Lyons promptly slipped out of the room. Along
with Nina Walling sat a yak-haired young man, and
in the rear of the car, another trendy couple.

Lyons returned not only with Nina Walling, but
also with her attendant Struwwelpeter. The latter,
viewed at closer quarters, seemed less youthful; he
was probably about thirty-five. Nina was tall, and
looked strangely sexless in a flowing, ankle-length
gown: a small face on a long neck over a draped,
stick-like figure. She had Walling's nose, in a more
delicate form, but otherwise her features were fine
and sharp. Her eyes were pale violet. They observed
Gently with contemptuous hauteur.

'You wished to talk to me about Adrian?' Her
voice resembled Walling's, but had a chilling preci-
sion.

Gently nodded woodenly. 'But I'd prefer to talk
to you on your own.'

'Oh—this is Ivan. You will want him too. He was
working with Adrian last week. Evidence of state of
mind, you know. From what I've read it could have
been suicide.'

Gently glanced at her companion. 'Ivan Webster?'

'Right on the button, fuzz,' the Struwwelpeter replied. He had bold, humourless grey eyes, and a
beak-like nose: avine features.

'So what was his state of mind?' Gently asked.

'Bloody,' Webster said. 'Extra bloody.' He nodded towards the script on the sofa. 'He hung enough re-write on me to keep me sweating for a week.'

'Would that be unusual?'

Webster eyed him. 'No. He was always a sod to work with. Only last week he was busting all records. Like there was something special eating him.'

'Do you know what it was?'

Webster paused. 'Is it a secret?'

'I'm asking you,' Gently said.

'Oh, it isn't a secret,' Nina Walling said impatiently. 'Not to me and not to Ivan.'

'Because we relate, you know,' Webster leered. 'The liberation thing. You catch it, fuzz?'

Gently hunched a shoulder. 'So now you can tell me.'

'It was his deal with Daddy,' Nina Walling said promptly. 'Daddy is having some trouble with his package tour business, and Adrian got uptight and wanted to pull out. Adrian was always in a twist about money. He couldn't freewheel with it like Daddy.'

'Stoll told you about it?'

'Of course not! Daddy told me about it, on Friday. But it would have worked out all right. Adrian knew he could trust Daddy, really.'

'When did you last see Stoll?'

'Midweek sometime. I think it was Wednesday.'

'Not since then?'

'No. We didn't live in each other's pockets.'

'Not the liberation thing?'

Webster chuckled sardonically, but Nina Walling seemed not at all put out.

'We related,' she said. 'The father–daughter thing. It was a liberation that Adrian needed.'

'And helpful to you?'

'Of course. What's wrong with people helping one another?'

'In this case it seems to have affected some other people.'

'Whom Adrian had been helping for a long time anyway.' She hesitated, her eyes firmly on Gently's. '*I* didn't want to cause them trouble,' she said. 'I wasn't bugging Adrian to unrelate with them. That was his decision entirely.'

'So he told you of his intentions?'

'Yes. He was going to make a clean break. I think it was largely that he'd grown away from Maryon. Which is something that happens all the time.'

'Did he mention any provisions for her?'

Nina Walling shook her head. 'But she had been living off him for years.'

'His will?'

She shook her head again. 'But I'm certain he would have seen her all right,' she said.

'He wasn't a bad bastard,' Webster murmured. 'Like just a bastard, period, period.'

Gently considered Webster expressionlessly. 'What was your relation with Stoll, precisely?' he said.

Webster laughed. 'I'm a scriptwriter,' he said. 'One of those people Adrian ate before breakfast. But I lived with it, fuzz. First and last, I worked with Adrian for four years. In a hateful way we kind of related. Like I read his mind better than most.'

'How long have you known Miss Walling?'

Webster double-took. 'Now you're getting naughty thoughts, fuzz. I didn't gas Adrian, though sometimes I might have done. Like someone else got in first.'

'You think it's a joke?' Gently said.

'*I* think it was suicide,' Webster said. 'Him getting in a twist thiswise, thatwise, and finding it kept adding up to zero. It's a soft way to go, sniffing gas, like going to sleep without setting the alarm. And Adrian was a loner, an upshut guy. As a character, I can see him wanting to bust out.'

'Have you ever been to Brayling?'

'Yah.'

'You know the forest?'

'I know bits.'

'Then let's hear what you were doing last week-end.'

Webster rolled his eyes to the ceiling. 'Fuzz,' he said, 'you are lovely. You are a very nice person. Give me time, and I could relate. But all last week-end I was in town.'

'Doing what in town?'

'Like first I was eating in the Centre canteen. That was after Adrian had blown, remember? Then I went home to work on the script.'

'Went where?'

'My flat in Battersea, just off Albert Bridge Road. After which I collected Nina from the Capri, and we had a drink, and I drove her home. Want me to go on?'

Gently said nothing.

'All of which I confirm,' Nina Walling said frostily.

'Oh, but he's so lovely,' Webster chanted. 'Get that Squaresville jaw. I'll have to use him, somewhere.'

'And now,' Nina Walling said, 'perhaps we can go— if you've finished with the corny questions. Have you finished?'

Gently shrugged. The two of them went out, Webster to wait in the car.

Lyons was staring uncertainly at Gently. 'Were you serious about that fellow, sir?' he asked.

Gently made a face. 'I don't know. Just that he seemed to be asking for a try-on.'

'I can't see any motive for him,' Lyons said doubtfully. 'Stoll would be worth more to him alive than
dead.'

'Still,' Gently said, 'you may as well check him.'
Lyons sighed to himself, very softly.

4

Latchford had changed in a number of ways since Gently was there a decade earlier. The main road now sliced through the north of the town, which put him at fault when he drove in. The industrial sector and the raw overspill estates had further encroached on the silent brecks: a more extensive urbation, though still wholly alien, still seeming at the frontiers, of a hostile land. But the change was most subtle in the old town, which apparently hadn't changed at all; where the same narrow, crooked, rather seedy streets spidered round the small market-place and the Regency town hall. Now it had a bruised, fading look, as though over-punished by traffic and people—still hanging on to its rigid identity, but growing ghostly, like the brecks. Latchford, the new technological community, was shaping this spectre in its midst: and raising along with it a strange question—who, in truth, was haunting whom?

But there was nothing ghostly about Metfield, who seemed a different man on his own patch. He came down the steps of the police station to welcome Gently with a confident hand. A press photographer recorded the event, while his colleague tried for a statement: Gently murmured generalities about a routine exchange and hastened into the station. Metfield bustled after him, full of buck. He ushered Gently into his office.

'No go at the other end, sir?'

Gently sighed and took a seat. 'I wouldn't exactly say that. Lyons is continuing his investigation.'

'But this Walling chap—you've cleared him?'

'Walling has given us an account of his movements. Lyons is checking it out now. It may be difficult to prove much against Walling.'

'That was my opinion all along, sir.' Metfield dropped happily behind his desk. 'It has to be someone who knows the forest. Nobody else is worth considering.'

'A local man.'

'No question, sir. Or someone who's lived round here for a while. And that's the cousin, Edwin Keynes. He's the only one who could have set it up.'

'With or without collaboration.'

'Yes, sir.' Metfield nodded vigorously. 'They're all in it, that's my belief—Keynes, her, the daughter, and the painter who's living with him. All we need now is a bit of luck, so that we can show they knew what Stoll had in mind for them.'

Gently crossed his legs cautiously. We can probably show that.'

'We can, sir?' Metfield's eyes sparkled excitedly.

'Walling coughed. He was a guest at Brayling Lodge the previous weekend. A row started when Stoll caught his cousin and Maryon Britton kissing. They revealed that they were aware of Stoll's relations with Miss Walling, and Stoll gave the Brittons notice to quit, and spoke of making a fresh will.'

'Then we've got them, sir!'

Gently grinned at the local man. 'Perhaps not quite.'

'But why not, sir? This Walling can't go back on his cough.'

'He might,' Gently said. 'But we can put pressure on him, so I don't think he will. But that still gives

us only motive and propinquity, neither of which are
hard evidence. Unless you can add something?'

Metfield did his swallowing trick, and shook his
head.

'So it isn't enough,' Gently said. 'Grounds for
strong suspicion, but that's all. We'll have to get
after them a bit harder, turn up some evidence that
will stick.' He paused. 'Did you process the pamphlet?'

'Yes, sir.' Metfield sounded glum. 'There's a fair
latent on it, a stranger, along with Stoll's and some
of ours. We sent a copy to C.R.O., but chummie isn't
on record.'

'Let me see it.'

Metfield opened a drawer, and passed a slim leaflet
to Gently. In fact, it consisted of a single buff sheet,
twice folded, like a map. On the cover was a woodcut
of a red squirrel, sitting alertly on a pine branch,
along with the titling: LATCHFORD FOREST / JUBILEE
FOREST TRAIL / Forestry Commission / 2½p. Gently
opened it. It commenced with a preamble about the
forest, then continued with notes on features of the
trail, numerically keyed to a plan at the back. 'Stop
No. 4' was the critical entry. A woodcut of badger
spoor was annexed to it. After some remarks on
natural regeneration the text continued thus:

> The belt of Scots Pine on your left is known
> locally as Mogi's Belt, after a dog called Mogi
> which was accidentally killed here during a
> pheasant shoot. Mogi's Belt, which is W.D. prop-
> erty, is strictly private, and notices warn you of
> unexploded bombs.
>
> The fence at this point is designed to exclude
> harmful herbivores, but one animal, the BAD-
> GER, is a good friend to the forester, since his
> diet includes insects which cause harm to the
> trees. He is a creature of strict habits, especially

in routes to and from his sett, so that once he has a path established he will use it in spite of obstacles placed across it. Thus, to avoid the continued expense of fence repairs, it was found necessary to install the gate you see here, which provides two-way access for badgers while discouraging rabbits and hares.

These two paragraphs had been marked with a red ballpen; and the plan had been similarly marked, where it showed the trail passing Mogi's Belt. Also drawn in was a small circle, presumably indicating the badger sett.

Gently laid the pamphlet on the desk. 'Where do you buy these?' he asked.

Metfield shrugged. 'You can buy them at the Forest Centre, or from self-service units at some of the car parks. But they have them here in town, too. One of the newsagents stocks them. I put a man on trying to trace this one, but he was beat before he started.'

'Let me see Stoll's personal effects.'

Metfield fetched a plastic bag from a locker. Among the bits and pieces was a Parker ballpen. Gently scribbled with it. Red.

Metfield stared at the red scribble. 'It doesn't prove anything,' he said. 'Stoll may have marked it up himself, but somebody must have told him where to put the circle.'

'He might have guessed where it went from the text.'

'That circle is near enough spot on.'

'So,' Gently shrugged. 'Someone told him. Gave him the pamphlet. Set it up.'

He checked through the rest of the effects, an expensive but oddly anonymous collection, as though Stoll had lately gone out with a thick bank roll and kitted himself out from scratch. Nothing personalized by wear, and a minimum of documents. A notebook, charmingly bound in crimson lambskin, contained only a handful of scribbled memos—'Shoot Ps. Wed.' 'Rs. Fri.' etc. It confirmed what Gently had seen at the flat, which was similarly expensive and impersonal— the pied-à-terre of a highly paid worker, with the tools of his trade, and little else. For example, no personal letters, but a batch of truly stupendous phone bills. While matters domestic and secretarial had been taken care of by agencies. Stoll had been a loner: outside his vocation, very little of him had overflowed.

Metfield produced the will. It was dated October, 1965, the year of Stoll's divorce and the purchase of Brawling. It left no doubt that at the time it was drawn, Maryon Britton stood high in Stoll's regard. Probably more than one-half of his estate was being willed to her, and away from his own child, while the bequests to her daughter and to Edwin Keynes cut a fat slice from the remainder. Stoll's ex-wife, Rosalind Rix, was conspicuously absent from the carve-up.

'Enough motive there, sir,' Metfield murmured, reading the will over Gently's shoulder.

'If they knew the size of it,' Gently grunted. 'And we've no reason yet to suppose they did.'

'He'd have told her at the time, sir. He was barmy about her.'

'He doesn't strike me as having been that sort of man.'

'At least he would have told her she was getting the house.'

But would he? They were dealing with Adrian Stoll.

Metfield's prize exhibit, the blue Volkswagen Dormobile, was locked away in an M/T garage. Its engine started first bang, and Metfield backed it into the yard. Predictably it was newish, immaculate and impersonal: another tool of Stoll's trade. It differed from standard in only one particular, being fitted with a second, heavy-duty battery, with an exterior take-off. This was apparently to power the floodlight, which was still packed in the vehicle, along with a camera-stand, portable flash and several cans of unused film. For the rest, one more Dormobile, smelling of soft fabric and curtaining, with a single sleeping-bag and pillow, and the makings of a mug of powdered coffee.

Metfield unbuttoned the roof and raised it until spring pegs locked the supports. Then he opened one of two large orange-perspex ventilators, showing how they gapped downwards when the roof was erected. Next he made up the bed, by drawing out hinged seat-cushions and sliding them laterally over the fitted cool-box; and finally fetched the gas bottle, with the hose attached, and fed the hose into the open ventilator. It dangled within eighteen inches of the head of the bed.

'Turn it on!' Gently called.

Metfield operated the valve. From the hose came a faint, serpent-like hiss and a garlic smell that seemed to scratch at the brain.

Metfield turned it off and came round to the side-door.

'Is that the original bottle?' Gently asked.

'Yes, sir,' Metfield said. 'It still had some gas in it. Larling turned it off when he found the van.'

'What can the suppliers tell us about that?'

'Well, not very much, sir,' Metfield admitted. 'We don't know if the bottle started full or if the valve was turned full on.'

'But if it was full, and full on?'

'They reckoned five hours, which would put the time it was turned on at two-thirty a.m. And that's about what you'd expect, sir. Chummie would have had to let Stoll settle down.'

Metfield next proceeded to demonstrate the gas stove, which popped up from behind the front passenger-seat; it had been found folded, but could not be folded unless a safety-tap was first turned off. A complete irrelevancy. All that signified was that green pipe dangling from the ventilator. Cheap, easy, non-violent: and with a little care, untraceable. A method for an amateur, for a squeamish operator, for a woman. Or a womanish man.

'Just thought I'd show you, sir,' Metfield said. 'You wouldn't need to go further, if you were planning suicide.'

'Put it away,' Gently shrugged. 'What I want to see now is where it was done.'

He left his Lotus in the yard and they drove out in a police Wolseley. Metfield was a careful, methodical driver who followed precisely the drill in the manual. They left Latchford by the Cross road and stole ahead at a steady fifty. Very soon they were clear of the houses and entering the fenceless stretches of the breck.

'Would this have been Stoll's route?' Gently asked.

Metfield nodded. 'Coming in from London. I haven't found anyone yet who saw him, but any other way would put on miles.'

'He would have been going through Latchford at around ten.'

'That's when a lot of traffic would have been leaving. But not so much of it going this way. He could have slipped by without anyone noticing.'

'What's over to the left?'

'That's the Battle Area, on the far side of those trees.'

'Was anything going on there at the weekend?'

Metfield shook his head. 'The Camp is closed for repairs.'

And if the military were absent there would be
nobody else on those wide, wasted acres, where cottage and farmhouse rotted and collapsed, and the
roads were vanishing again, into the brecks.

They passed a straggle of native pines, their flaky
boles purplish-red, and headed for the long palisade
of the forest, lying trim and alert under the sun. The
mass of the trees were evergreen conifers, Scots,
Corsican and Douglas, but they were skirted with
deciduous saplings, beech, maple, larch and sycamore.
Then, as the Wolseley left the main road, they entered an avenue of great oak and beech trees, arboreal
patriarchs, set wide apart, so that each followed each
in majestic spectacle. Their sheer size and complexity
of foliated architecture was a surprise and an astonish-
ment: one felt one had never really seen trees till
now, and that now one was seeing too many too
quickly.

'You should come here in the autumn,' Metfield
murmured complacently. 'I usually make a trip or
two out here, then. Some of the colours you wouldn't
believe, much less put a name to. It's a different
world.'

The road here was spaced with wide verges, letting in sun and a fret of sky. But beyond the great
trees lay the regiments of pines, dim, motionless and
enclosing. Truly a different world. Their deep, pillared glades had an electric presence. At their feet
grew dull snowberry and purple-leaved bramble, with
the occasional pallor of white campion. And the
dividing rides, with their painted signatures, also departed into enclosed dimness, with verges rough with
tangled grass, and flecked with campions, and the
chalked blue of bugloss. Here, no doubt, the deer
lived, though the forest offered no sight or sound of
them. It was simply still, and silent, with its own
silence; where the trees lived, in tree time.

They turned left into Warren Ride, along which ran a regular though bumpy track. Metfield slowed the Wolseley, not so much because of the bumps as to avoid raising a cloud of soft, reddish dust. A car approaching them without this precaution was trailing a dense and billowing banner; after it passed, for the next hundred yards, they were seeing the trees through a rusty haze.

'The bastard!' Metfield exclaimed. 'One day I'll do a joker for that.'

'It'll be chalk dust,' Gently said. 'Coloured with iron. Does it occur anywhere else round here?'

Metfield pondered a moment. 'No,' he said. 'The tracks are mostly marl or gravel.'

'There was orange stain on the tyres of the caravette.'

Metfield nodded. 'There'd been rain,' he said. 'It was still puddly on Sunday, along by the fence.'

'Just along there?'

Metfield kept nodding. 'And I need my backside kicking, sir,' he said. 'But perhaps it isn't too late now. We haven't had any rain since.'

'It's too late for Walling,' Gently said. 'I saw his car in town yesterday. It had been recently washed and polished. Though that could be a pointer, too.'

'Yes, sir,' Metfield said, through his teeth. And went on nursing the car down the ride.

On the wide verge to the left a number of cars and caravettes were parked, and now and then, as they passed a crossride, they caught glimpses of distant strollers; then the verge ended, the trees encroached, and the track became even rougher, ending at last in a thinned-out glade, where two or three other cars had penetrated.

'This is where we turn off, sir.'

Metfield dropped the Wolseley into second. Short of the glade by about fifty yards was an intersecting ride to the right. At the junction was a stake marked with painted arrowheads, which the Forestry used to indicate their trails, and recent tracks of vehicles were visible in moist leaf-mould at the entrance of the ride. Metfield turned into it. At once they were in the deep shade of the trees. On one hand were the grey boles of Douglas pines, on the other the pinker shafts of Corsicans. The track was broken by outcrops of chalk and gulches of partly dried mud; and there were carpets of polished needles which set the Wolseley's wheels spinning. Metfield pressed on gamely. After a few twists and turns, the track brought them to a view of the sky on the left, where a belt of majestic Scots pines stood a little clear of a meshed fence.

'Mogi's Belt.' Metfield stopped the car before they bore off along the line of the fence. 'This used to be a sporting estate, once, sir. They planted these belts to give cover to the pheasants.'

'And behind that fence is the Battle Area?'

'Yes, sir. It runs right through to Ickburgh. Only the army never come within a mile of this place—they hold their manoeuvres round the old villages.'

Gently grunted and stared at the fence, which was plainly not of recent origin. Rust was gnawing at the wire mesh and separating in flakes from the metal stakes. Had Stoll needed to be told it was safe to trespass here, or had he simply gone in, taking his chance? Certainly, a man who was seeking badgers might have picked up a hint from the Forestry pamphlet!

'So where's the gate?'

Metfield set off again. Now the track ran straight, following the fence. Within a hundred yards they came to the gate; and beside it a Land-Rover, in which a man sat smoking.

* * *

'This is Larling, sir.'

The man had got down, and was methodically stubbing out his cigarette. He was dressed in a crumpled tweed jacket and jeans, and an open-necked khaki shirt. A solid-looking man, about forty, his face tanned and roughened.

'He's the Forestry ranger who found the body.'

Larling came up slowly to the car. He nodded to Metfield and glanced keenly at Gently. He was shredding the cigarette-butt between thick fingers. He gestured to the pines with his head.

'We've got a peeper in there,' he said. 'I've been parked here twenty minutes. I've caught a couple of looks at him since then.'

Metfield peered into the trees. 'How do you mean, a peeper?'

'He was about when I got here,' Larling said. 'I heard him backing away through the section. But I could hear he hadn't gone very far. So I just lit a fag and sat quiet.'

'Know who it is?'

Larling shook his head. 'He didn't come close enough for that. I saw him once over by that snowberry, then again further this way, near the elder. A youngster, I thought. He was wearing a dark shirt, maybe blue. That's all I can tell you.'

Metfield fingered his jowls. 'Probably just a snooper. There's several cars back in the Ride.'

Larling nodded. 'I thought I'd tell you,' he said. 'I reckon he'll have slid off now, with you turning up.'

They climbed out of the car into the feathered sunlight and the cool, resin odour of the pines. The gate in the fence was also rusted, and the paint of its warning notice dull. Its chain and padlock hung unshackled. Gently tested the action of the latter. The hinged arm moved very stiffly, required strength to spring it when closed. He let it dangle again.

'Is this how you found it when you got here, twenty minutes ago?'

'That's right,' Larling said. 'I haven't touched it. The gate was shut, but the chain was hanging.'

Gently looked at Metfield. 'How did you leave it?'

Metfield goggled. 'Chained, of course! That cheeky so-and-so has been poking round there. Larling must have scared him off.'

'Interesting,' Gently said. He gave his attention to the gate. It was constructed of welded angle-iron, about eight feet high, with the wire mesh attached to it by steel clips. The clips were inserted all around the frame and rusted points stuck out meanly. They stuck out on the opening edge of the gate. And on one was a snag of dark fibres.

Metfield, who'd been watching, sucked in breath.

'That'll be off chummie's sleeve,' he said. 'And like as not he scratched his arm—he must have come out of there in a hurry.'

'This wasn't here earlier?' Gently said.

'No, sir,' Metfield said. 'We'd been all over it. So now I'm beginning to wonder if he's just a snooper, or whether we shouldn't be getting after him.'

Larling spat a shred of tobacco. 'You'll need some dogs for that,' he said. 'He'll have had ten minutes' start, anyway, and if he's got a car he'll be away.'

They both stared at Gently, who was stooping to examine the ground by the gate; but the ground was carpeted with matted grass: nothing useful to be had there.

'We'll leave it,' he said. 'Perhaps our friend will turn up again, if his curiosity is so keen.'

'Yes, sir,' Metfield said humbly.

Gently drew a plastic envelope from his wallet.

Larling showed them the badger gate, a simple contrivance that relied on the weight of the shutter for its operation, coupled with the circumstance that hares and rabbits would be shy of pushing against it, while a badger would unhesitatingly shoulder it open. Then they returned to the fence gate, and went through it into the confusion of underbrush and self-seeded saplings, from which the sunned, rosy pillars of the pines rose massively to their dark crowns of felted needles.

The tracks of the caravette were plain to follow through the snowberry and bracken. Twigs were snapped, fronds spreadeagled, and leaf-mould scattered by spinning wheels. The tracks bore right, avoiding one of the pines, and passed under a screen of young birch and elder; then they climbed over a brackeny bank and lurched down into a dell.

'Here we are,' Larling said. 'Here's the place where I found him. And I reckon he'd never have driven in here unless he'd known where he was coming.'

Gently shrugged and advanced into the dell. The extent of Stoll's information showed here yet more plainly. There had been no manoeuvring of the caravette; it had been driven at once to its parked position. The tracks, though disturbed by subsequent trampling, remained sufficiently to tell the story, along with deep indentations in the leaf-mould at the spot to which Larling had pointed. From there they proceeded in a firm lock, showing where the police had driven the van away.

'Where's the badger sett?'

'Under that beech. So like he'd have his headlights facing straight at it.'

'Wouldn't that upset the badgers?'

Larling shook his head. 'Not if he was quiet. Lights don't seem to bother them.'

The beech was old, a natural curiosity, with four stems rising from a rampart of roots; rainwater lay in a basin between the stems, and the boughs above

were strangely intergrown. Around the roots grew
anaemic nettles, concealing the mouth of an im-
pregnable tunnel.

'That's where they are,' Larling mused. 'And I
reckon that's where they've been for a century. Nobody's going to dig them out of that. And I'm to ask
you not to mention badgers to the press.'

Gently stared at the tunnel. 'So who would know
they were here?'

'Not nobody should, by rights,' Larling said. 'This
is W.D. property, and nobody shouldn't set foot in
here. But we know, of course. Between you and me,
we've been in here sizing up the timber. But we'd
never mention that sett to anyone. It'd be as much as
our jobs were worth.'

'Then how *did* Stoll come by the information?'

Larling looked blank. 'That's been puzzling me too.
I've had a word with one or two of the other men, but
Mr Stoll didn't get it from them. I'm the only one he's
ever approached, and that was a time back, about the
deer. I took him up eighty-four, which is a mile from
here. There was no mention of Mogi's Belt or badgers.'

'Would you perhaps get poachers in here, after
pheasants?'

Larling looked doubtful. 'That's not very likely.
The pheasants don't breed this way any more. It's
where there's shoots you find the pheasants.'

'Yet somehow . . . he *knew*.'

'That's right,' Larling agreed. 'I can only reckon he
nosed it out by himself.'

'Except someone else knew too,' Metfield put in
stubbornly. 'The chummie who followed him in with
a gas bottle.'

Gently took a few steps round the beech and pushed
through the saplings and nettles beyond it. A dozen
yards brought him to the edge of the belt and to a
steep bracken-and-bramble-defended slope. Below it

lay shaking bog-land, stippled with common orchids, and what looked like buckbean; then, a quarter of a mile off, the russet sweep of the brecks, with a lacing of dwarf birches, and a few sad, deformed pines. No track, no passage that way—with or without a hefty gas bottle! The bracken and the brambles flourished undisturbed, and no plunging feet had printed the green mire.

He turned back into the trees. Metfield and Larling stood where he had left them, near the beech: two figures that seemed to accentuate the secluded loneliness of the spot. About them, the wilderness of underbush and the columns of great trees, so indifferent and abstracted from this temporary restlessness of men. And into that lone place, dimmed by night, the blue caravette had found its way, to settle so certainly in its place, its driver careless of the still spirits round him. Because he was familiar with the location? No. The marked-up plan determined that. If Stoll had reconnoitred the spot previously the marking-up would not have been necessary. Stoll had been briefed, and briefed in detail, by someone who *had* made a reconnaisance: no further doubt was possible. The killing had been coldly and meticulously planned.

About to move forward again, he hesitated, catching a movement in his peripheral vision. He kept his head steady but turned his eyes, seeking a focus in the distant underbrush. A leafed twig moved furtively, revealing a faint pallor behind: then it moved again, and the pallor became a face and intent eyes. Involuntarily, Gently turned his head: the leaves sprang back and the face vanished.

'Come on!' he shouted to Metfield and Larling, and jumped down into the dell.

'But what—what—?' Metfield gaped.

'Our snooper—and this time we're going to catch him!'

He raced across the dell and pounded over the
brackeny bank. The snooper had been lurking in the
direction of the gate, and probably only a short distance inside it. The gate, left closed, now stood ajar.
Gently shoved through it and stood panting. The ride
stretched straight and empty on the line of the fence,
in both directions. Metfield came puffing up beside
him, and Larling, running easily.

'Which way now?' Metfield gasped.

'Quiet!' Gently snapped. 'Listen!'

In a moment they heard it: a quick, stealthy rus-
tling, deep in the section of Douglas pine.

'Spread out!' Gently commanded.

They charged into the section, Metfield running
left, Larling right. The section, composed of mature
timber, was plentifully furnished with the ubiquitous
snowberry. Now their quarry had dispensed with caution. They could hear him crashing and plunging
ahead of them. By luck or design he was crossing the
tree-lines in a diagonal, which kept him concealed behind the shutter of the boles. Twice only Gently
glimpsed him, a lithe, flying figure, bounding deer-like
through the snowberry. A youngster, certainly; on the
tall side; his dark shirt a bottle green.

'Reckon he's heading for Warren,' Larling panted.
'And I'll tell you another thing—he's fit!'

'Can't we head him off?' Gently gasped.

'No we can't. And if he's got a car, we've had him!'

It was humiliating. Three middle-aged men, slowly
running themselves to a standstill: while chummie
steamed busily away from them, his sounds growing
ever more distant. And nothing to be done! Gently
plunged on savagely, his feet dragging in bramble and
snowberry. Chummie had reduced them to making
motions—they couldn't catch him, and couldn't not
try.

'There's Warren—through there!'

Sharp sunlight ahead, and the glowing green of deciduous leaves. Through his sweat Gently spotted the dark shirt bend low under the boughs of saplings, and vanish. He nerved himself to a last, lumbering sprint. The interval to the sunlight seemed to stretch like elastic. Then he heard the brisk clunk of a car door, followed immediately by the revving of an engine.

'Something small . . . a Mini . . . an Imp!'

He bullocked his way through whipping twigs of sycamore. And too late again. All he arrived in time for was the comet-tail of red dust, fingering fast down the track.

'Oh the bastard, the bastard!' Metfield sobbed, tottering out beside Gently. 'I'll have the next one for sure, who does that!'

And he collapsed with dignity, to wipe his sweat.

5

Metfield, like Setters before him, had booked Gently
into the Sun. It was still the best hotel in Latchford,
though now enlarged and shyly in-trend. Its pale,
aloof, but agreeable face had once met the coaches ar-
riving from London; as they crossed the bridge, after
the perils of the heath, they saw first this haven, waiting to welcome them. Well, the bypass had ended all
that, while at the same time mysteriously increasing
the town traffic. But the Sun had survived this technological alchemy. It remained the place into which
the locals booked Gently.

Over lunch, to which Gently had invited him, Metfield found the Yard man a silent companion. He ate
with a stolid, impenetrable composure, and stared out
of the window between courses. They took coffee in
the lounge, where Gently lit his pipe, and Metfield a
modest Panatella; but it was not till the second cup
that Gently condescended to unbend.

Then he regarded the local man with a twinkling,
hazel eye.

'Do you think we should contemplate a Third
Force?'

Metfield's Panatella slipped a notch. 'How do you
mean, sir?'

Gently blew a ring. 'The situation is in balance,
and a Third Force would be the classic solution. On
what we have I don't fancy Walling, and I'm not con-

vinced that I shall fancy the tribe at Brayling. Which leaves us with our Wild Man of the Woods. Who certainly seemed equipped with local knowledge.'

'But, sir!' Metfield gazed with rounding eyes. 'Sir, that chummie could still have been just a snooper. But Keynes and the woman are residents here—they'd have local knowledge, if anyone would.'

Gently shook his head. 'There's a simple objection that applies both to them and to Walling. Having that local knowledge was not enough: they had still to impart it to Stoll and to get him to act on it. But neither Walling nor the others were in Stoll's good books. They couldn't suddenly cut in with friendly information. Stoll would have suspected something directly—if only that they were trying to get rid of him for the weekend.'

Metfield gulped unhappily. 'But they could have planted it—somehow!'

Gently shaped another ring. 'I've been trying to think how. And always I keep coming back to this: Stoll must have trusted the person who told him. They would necessarily have had quite a long conversation, involving a detailed briefing and the marking of the pamphlet. Stoll knew he could rely on the information he was given, and had no reason to suspect an ulterior motive. So it had to be a familiar acquaintance, and one currently on excellent terms with Stoll.'

'But Keynes or Maryon Britton could have put him up to it, sir. He didn't need to know what it was about.'

'He would have to have known,' Gently said. 'Or perhaps he wouldn't have kept their names out of it. It's a possibility, though rather remote as far as Keynes and Britton are concerned. On the other hand it might fit Walling, who probably had a wider spectrum of shared acquaintances. Or—we can postulate a Third Force.'

Metfield dragged on his cigar dejectedly. 'Do you have a sus, sir?'

Gently shrugged. 'Better call it an area of mild interest. It doesn't add up to a genuine sus, because at the moment we're stumped for a motive.'

'But it's connected with chummie who was keeping an eye on us?'

'There could possibly be a connection. Or possibly I could be following a bum hunch.' Gently's eyes twinkled. 'Which is why I'm putting it up to you.'

Metfield shook his head and looked in his coffee.

'You don't like it?' Gently said.

Metfield breathed deeply. 'Not without motive, sir. Because that's what we've got here in big handfuls.' He looked squarely at Gently. 'So it's a queer one, sir, and we can't quite figure how they worked it. But all the rest adds up to Keynes and the lady, and that's where I'm going to keep my money.'

Gently nodded. 'Right,' he said. 'Then we'd better see if we can prove it.'

Metfield ground his cigar into an ashtray. 'Yes, sir,' he said. 'That's what we'll do.'

They drove out by the same road as earlier, across the brecks and into the forest, but this time passed Warren Ride and continued along the avenue of great trees. The road ran straight and smooth, logged by the regular passing of the rides. A few cars were parked on the grassy verges, but singly, and spaced far apart. At length they came to a left turn, where shaggy fields of arable encroached on the forest; and leaving the trees by degrees, reached the first cottages of West Brayling village.

'This is the back way in,' Metfield said. 'Very convenient for the forest. You can slip along here from the Lodge and never go near the village.'

'Who lives in the cottages?' Gently asked.

'Farmworkers, mostly,' Metfield said. 'I've had a word with them. One of them remembers a car going by, early Sunday morning.'

'But which, of course, he didn't see,' Gently said.

Metfield twitched a beefy shoulder.

Now the village was spreading ahead of them, a cluster of red roofs hiding among trees; with the crisp tower and crocketed spire of a medieval church breaking the skyline. But while it was still distant they came abreast of a serpentine red-brick wall, above which reared a single, enormous cedar, and the tops of ornamental shrubs.

'Here we are, sir,' Metfield muttered. 'This is what Stoll was leaving in his will.'

He turned the car through an arched brick gateway, of which the wrought-iron gates stood open. They proceeded along a gravel drive, between trim hedges of copper beech, and came shortly to a sweep at the side of a red-brick Georgian house.

'Like it, sir?'

Gently grunted and got down from the Wolseley. The house, though not large, had the insouciant graciousness of things Georgian. On each side of a simple, pillared porch ranged four deep sash windows, matched by shallower ones above, and by dormers above those. The roof was of blue glazed pantiles, broken by ornamented chimney-breasts, and the gables were Dutch: semicircular brick screens plumped by lesser segments at the corners. To the rear of the house was a stable-block, overshadowed by oaks and copper beeches. Before it extended a lawn with colourful side-beds, bounded by the serpentine wall and the beech hedging. Doors, windows, stood open in the still sunlight. French doors had been fitted to one ground-floor window.

'Yes—you wanted something?'

A girl had come to the side door, where she stood

staring at Gently with hostility. She was aged in her late teens and had a glinting helmet of ash-blonde hair. Her face was finely-featured but narrow, with cheeks thinning below the cheekbone; there was a droop in her small mouth, and a hint of shadow beneath each eye.

'Miss Britton?' Gently inquired.

'That's my name,' she said bleakly. Then her eyes went past him to Metfield in the car. 'Oh,' she said. 'You're another policeman.'

'Chief Superintendent Gently,' Gently said.

'And of course, you want to talk to Mother.'

'To your mother and yourself,' Gently said.

Miss Britton stared at him with passionate blue eyes. She went inside: slamming the door. Gently turned to Metfield, who made a face.

'You'll find her a difficult one, sir,' he said. 'She gave me some cheek when I was round here earlier.'

'Do we know who her father was?'

Metfield shrugged. 'A reporter I spoke to said he was an actor. Her mother was properly married and all that. The lady was a widow when Stoll took up with her.'

'What happened to the man?'

'Suicide, they say. He took an overdose of pills.' Metfield looked thoughtful. 'That kid has a background.'

'So has her mother,' Gently said.

Miss Britton reappeared.

'Very well,' she said. 'Mother will see you. And perhaps you will leave your car in the yard. Out here, it may inconvenience visitors.'

They followed her in. She took them down a narrow passage, leading to a central hall with an elegant staircase; then through an ivory-painted panelled door into a long, spacious drawing-room. It was furnished expensively. The floor was laid with a Persian carpet of extravagant area. Grouped about it was a Regency suite, comprising a long sofa and eight matching chairs. Two fine cabinets of the same period were set one each side of the elaborate hearth, and contained a collection of Chelsea figures such as one rarely saw outside a large museum. The principal picture was a Wilson, apparently an original, depicting a Thames scene at evening; but there were ten or a dozen contemporary pictures, including a sketch in oils by Constable. Near the door stood a Dutch bureau-book-case, its shelves dull with original board bindings; and another opposite, at the far end of the room, containing bindings of morocco, calf and vellum. Small Sheraton display-cases alternated with the larger furniture; they exhibited collections of watches and silver-and-enamel trifles; while the deep drop-ceiling had been enriched by a frieze of blue, green, white and black Wedgwood plaques. It was a room the contents of which were worth probably twice the value of the property; and which had not a single human touch, except a brash Melamine coffee-table, strewn with women's magazines.

'These are the gentlemen.'

Miss Britton crossed to the sofa and dropped on one end of it, with elaborate unconcern. At the other end sat an older woman, wearing a smartly cut trouser suit. It didn't quite become her: perhaps her figure was a little too full; or it might have been that the straw colour failed to complement her auburn-blonde hair. She had a soft-modelled, heart-shaped face with a trace of a snub nose, a pretty, dimpling mouth and large, appealing, warm-brown eyes. Her complexion was clear and fresh. She was wearing no make-up.

'You are the Chief Superintendent?'

Gently bowed slightly. 'Mrs Britton?'

'Well!' A dimple formed. 'In my profession we don't use that title.'

'But you are Mrs Britton?'

'Yes.' The dimple went slack. Also the eyes, which had begun to soften, became tight again, wary.

'I'm investigating the death of Mr Stoll.'

'Yes, I suppose we can take that for granted.'

'In the course of my inquiries I have had a conversation with Oscar Walling.'

'Oscar?' Her tone was contemptuous.

'He described a visit he made here recently. In view of what he told me, I have to ask you one or two questions.'

Her eyes stared at him unwinkingly: large, frank, but now hard. Then she composedly folded her hands in her lap: smooth, immaculately manicured hands.

'Do take a seat,' she said. 'You may as well be comfortable in your work. I would offer you a drink, too. But no doubt you don't feel able to accept it.'

Gently shrugged and took a Regency chair, which neither looked comfortable nor was so. Metfield also sat. Mrs Britton had ignored him: alongside Gently he ranked as supernumerary. Miss Britton ignored both Metfield and Gently. She sat swinging a leg and gazing through the French window.

'So what are these questions, Chief Superintendent?'

'Do you have a burglar-alarm system, Mrs Britton?'

Mrs Britton checked, her brows lifting slightly. Then she said: 'I would have thought the Inspector could have told you.'

Gently silenced Metfield with his hand. 'You tell me.'

'Very well. Of course we have. You can't know very much about Adrian if you suppose he would have left this stuff unprotected. We have both a closed circuit and a trembler system, connected with the police station at Latchford. When it's switched on you have only to breathe for it to sound like a general alarm at a fire-station.'

'Mr Stoll seems to have valued these trinkets.'

'Mr Stoll was very well aware of their value.'

'Perhaps some of them are genuine? That Wilson picture?'

'You may take it for granted they are very genuine.'

'Then it is quite a valuable collection, at today's prices.'

'At today's or yesterday's, Superintendent.'

'And the house? At today's prices?'

Mrs Britton opened her mouth. And closed it again.

'Then, of course, there is the sum in cash,' Gently said. 'Possibly greater than the minimum figure quoted. And one or two subsidiary matters. No doubt a valuer can give us the true picture.'

He reached out his hand, into which Metfield placed a briefcase he had brought in hugged under his arm. The briefcase was made of black morocco and bore the monogram '*A.S.*' in flowing gilt capitals. Gently laid it on his knees, monogram up. Mrs Britton's eyes stared at it fascinatedly.

'Stoll had this with him when he died,' Gently said.

There was a little gasp from Miss Britton, who had turned from contemplating the lawn.

'It rather puzzled us. It seemed an unlikely thing for a man to take with him when he was photographing wild life. But then we had assistance from Mr Walling, who suggested a plausible explanation.'

Mrs Britton's hands jerked. 'Is it . . . his will?'

Gently paused. 'Is it, Mrs Britton?'

She bit her lip. 'Isn't that what you're leading up to, with all this talk of values and money?'

Gently shook his head. 'It could be a valuation list. Mr Stoll would need one for insurance purposes. In fact, I understand one is lodged with his solicitors. Why do you ask if this is a will?'

'Because . . . because——!'

'You were expecting him to bring a will with him?'

Her brown eyes flashed furiously. 'There was a will. We knew there was. Is there anything strange about that?'

'You knew there was a will?'

'Yes—yes! And so would anyone who knew Adrian.'

'But you knew of the existence of *this* will.'

'Yes, all right. Yes, I knew!'

Gently snapped open the briefcase. 'Then, naturally, you would know of some of its provisions. The bequests to Mr Keynes and your daughter. And the forty-five thousand to yourself.'

'Not forty-five thousand!'

'Not?' Gently sounded mildly surprised. 'Perhaps I read the clause hurriedly. Don't hesitate to correct me.'

'Ohh!'

Mrs Britton jumped to her feet and went to stand at the French windows, with her back to Gently. She stood defiantly, her feet apart, her hands clasped tautly in front of her: a little regal. A slant of sunlight set her auburn hair in a blaze.

'Now ask me some questions,' Miss Britton drawled, her eyes fixed distantly on the Wilson. 'Ask me about gas. I know a lot about it. I read it all up in a magazine.'

'Jenny, be quiet,' her mother rapped.

'But this is terribly important,' Miss Britton said. 'One of us should know something about gas, or we won't fit in with the police theory.'

'I won't tell you again, Jenny!'

'For example,' Miss Britton drawled. 'The gas we use over here is butane. But on the Continent they prefer propane, because it freezes at a lower temperature. They are equally poisonous, however.'

'Jenny!' her mother turned fiercely to confront her.

'Oh, let's have it in the open,' Miss Britton said contemptuously. 'He's better at the cat-and-mouse game than we are.'

Mrs Britton glared dangerously at her daughter for a moment, then decorously but emphatically resumed her seat. Miss Britton continued to gaze at the Wilson. Though she was trembling a very little.

'When did you learn about this gas?' Gently asked her.

Miss Britton shrugged exaggeratedly. 'I have to admit it was only yesterday. I bought a camping magazine in Latchford, because it had an exhaustive article on bottled gas. A natural interest, wouldn't you say? Of course, I read it through enthralled.'

'Yesterday?'

'Isn't that sad? But you'll have only mine and Lawrence's word for it.' She hesitated. 'Oh, and in passing, it wasn't us who gassed Adrian.'

'Oh, my God!' Mrs Britton exclaimed, her eyes lifting to the moulded ceiling.

'I am glad to hear it,' Gently said. 'Perhaps now we can return to this matter of the will.'

He drew the document from the briefcase and loosened the tape that secured it. Mrs Britton eyed him bitterly.

'All right,' she said. 'No need to go on. I knew what I was supposed to be getting because Adrian told me at the time he made it. I knew also what Jenny would get, though I didn't know then about Edwin. That was something Adrian mentioned when he was bawling us out, the last time he was here.

Which no doubt was what Oscar told you. Oscar has no reason to love us.'

'You knew that those bequests were about to be rescinded?'

She looked at him steadily. 'Yes.'

Gently nodded. 'Thank you for saving time. Perhaps you will give me your account of that last week-end.'

Mrs Britton drew a long breath. 'First, you'd better know how I stood with Adrian. For these last few years I've been just his housekeeper. There has been nothing else in it at all. I knew it wouldn't last for ever and I didn't much depend on what you're holding. He was on the rebound when he made that, but it was all over in two or three years. I suppose I was a fool to carry on, but I wanted it to last till Jenny was through school. And I'd lost my contacts with the theatre. It wouldn't have been easy for me to start again.' She threw Gently a glance.

'Were those your only reasons?'

'You may add to them my natural inertia. This is a pleasant place to live. I don't look forward to returning to town.'

'Or, perhaps, leaving friends?'

The glance was longer. 'Naturally, I have acquaintances here.'

'Just acquaintances?'

Her mouth tightened. Her hands crept together again on her lap.

'Oh, he knows,' Miss Britton said softly. 'You may as well come clean, Mother. Dear Edwin has always been an uncle to me. It won't be traumatic if he becomes my father.'

'Be quiet!' her mother snapped.

'Just helping out,' Miss Britton said. 'I think he's dreamy.' She leaned back on the sofa, clasping one of her graceful knees.

Mrs Britton's eyes were smouldering. 'Very well,' she jerked to Gently. 'So you know. Edwin has always been a good friend. It was he who put Adrian on to this place.'

Gently hunched. 'How long had he been more than a good friend?'

'I don't think I need to answer that question.'

'Then I'll put it another way, Mrs Britton. How long since Stoll began to take notice?'

'He never did.' Her stare was tight. 'By then, Adrian couldn't have cared less. He'd have been a fool not to suspect about Edwin, but if he did he never showed it. He simply didn't care. When he'd finished with me, there were plenty of other women for him to turn to. From his point of view, it was probably convenient that I had taken up with his cousin.'

'And this was the situation on the last weekend.'

She checked. 'Substantially, yes.'

'He showed no disapproval?'

She pulled on her hands. 'No. Or none that counted for anything.'

'So then what was the row about?'

'I thought Oscar had told you that,' she said bitterly. 'It was about Adrian wanting to clear me out to make room for his new love, Nina Walling. Of course, it *started* about me and Edwin. Adrian had to have something to cue him in. But if you have talked to Oscar you'll know well enough that it was really about his precious daughter.' She paused, her eyes sparkling. 'Who is a promiscuous bitch, to my certain knowledge. She was using Adrian to sleep her way to the big time. But he either couldn't or wouldn't see it.'

'Though of course, she can act,' Miss Britton murmured. 'And may have other skills. Like ways with gas.'

'Be quiet,' her mother said automatically.

Miss Britton was quiet; she watched the Wilson.

'So the row was about Nina Walling,' Gently said. 'I understand it became heated.'

Mrs Britton took a fresh grip on her hands. 'You'll have heard all that from Oscar.'

'Still, I would like to hear it from you.'

'Then it's true. It was a vile row. It had been brewing up for years. Adrian despised me. I'd simply put up with it. But last Sunday week it all came out.'

'It was the final break.'

'Yes, it was. We could never have gone on after that. Things were said that couldn't be forgiven, even if either of us had wanted to try.'

'And you were given marching orders.'

Her mouth twisted. 'It wasn't quite as abrupt as that. He had an audience, remember, he had to temper his callousness a bit. Also, being Adrian, he wanted us to sweat on it, to anticipate the chop. So our doom was postponed while he went to sharpen the axe.'

'But he left you in no doubt of his intentions.'

She shook her head. 'I don't deny it. Edwin thought there was a chance of him cooling off, but I can't pretend to have had any hopes.'

'You would have had to quit this house.'

'Yes.'

'You would have lost any allowance he was making you.'

'Yes.'

'And this document, which is worth a fortune to you, was going to be destroyed before your eyes.'

Mrs Britton's face was grim. 'I see you are beginning to know Adrian,' she said.

'But none of this happened,' Gently said. 'You are still mistress of Brayling Lodge. And now it may belong to you, along with the contents, and a substantial sum in investments. Because Adrian Stoll died, quietly and without violence, not more than three miles from this place. A few hours before this will was destroyed, and before his intentions could take effect. When you, I understand, had no other alibi than what can be given you by two interested parties. Isn't that so?'

Her colour had drained suddenly, as though controlled by a switch. Her eyes were very large: her fingers white at the knuckle.

'Are you—charging me with killing him?'

'We know a car used this back road at the critical time.'

'Oh God! It wasn't mine.'

'When was the last time you drove your car past Mogi's Belt?'

'I? Never! I'd never heard of the place.'

'The track leads out of Warren Ride.'

'No—I don't know it.'

'There is a Forestry Trail along it.'

She shook her head, trembling, stupid.

'Your car has never been there?'

'No—no.'

'Think carefully, Mrs Britton.'

'Oh, no, never!'

'I would like the key of your garage, please.'

The effort of rising seemed almost too much for her and she hung on shakily, clutching the sofa; but then the buzz of a car engine sounded in the drive, proceeding past the house towards the yard. Mrs Britton sank back in the sofa.

'Oh, thank heavens! It's Edwin and Lawrence.'

'I would still like the key, please,' Gently said.

Silently, Miss Britton got up and fetched some keys.

In the yard a red Hillman Super Imp stood parked alongside the Police Wolseley. A man was leaning against it, leisurely filling his pipe from a deerskin pouch. He was aged near fifty, about five feet eleven, and dressed in an open-necked brown shirt and blue jeans; he had broad cheekboned features with a handsome profile, and a mane of untidy, greying, brown hair. He looked up smilingly as Gently approached, but went on carefully packing his pipe. Gently ran his finger along the roof of the Imp. His finger came away red. He showed it to the man.

The man chuckled. 'Dust from Warren Ride,' he said. 'That's the only place where the chalk surfaces—chalk of that colour, anyway.'

'You were there this morning?'

'Not I. I was seated at my typewriter, ill at ease.' He struck a light. I'm Edwin Keynes,' he said. 'And you'll be talent sent down from town.'

Gently grunted. 'So who was driving the car?'

'Probably Lawrence,' Keynes said, puffing. 'He borrowed it to do some shopping in Latchford. Though of course, the dust may not be today's.'

'And the stain on the tyres?' Gently said.

'Has to be older,' Keynes smiled. 'We've had no rain here for above a week, and Warren Ride dries out quite quickly.'

'But not the track that goes by Mogi's Belt.'

'A touch,' Keynes smiled. 'I know it well. But there are ruts enough in Warren Ride. No need to look further for the source of the stains.'

Gently stared at him. Keynes had a soft, cultivated, accentless voice. His brown eyes were flecked with gold: they returned Gently's stare amusedly. He nodded to the keys in Gently's hand.

'You'll have no luck there, I'm afraid,' he said. 'I happen to know Jenny washed the car yesterday. Shampoo and set. Very thorough.'

'You seem to know so many things,' Gently said.

Keynes nostrilled smoke. 'That's my profession.'

'Perhaps they include who killed your cousin?'

Keynes laughed aloud and reached his hand for the keys.

Gently gave them to him. Keynes unlocked the padlock that secured the coach-house doors. He set them wide. Sun stabbed into the gloom and reflected from the panels and bumpers of a maroon Sunbeam Rapier. It had been not only washed but polished and leathered: the gear was standing on a bench by the wall; and a dribble of water lay beneath a coiled hose which was neither green nor ribbed, but clear plastic.

'Done yesterday evening,' Keynes grinned. 'Lawrence gave her a hand. Shall I run it out for you?'

Gently shrugged. If the tyres had been stained, they certainly were not so now. Possibly there was deposit left in the tread, but it would need expert examination to discover it; and deposit in the tread was no indication that the car had been driven beyond Warren Ride. He opened a door. The carpets were immaculate. No helpful smears on door panels or seat backs. In the boot, the same: a virgin carpet, free of all marks from heavy objects.

'Here—what about this?' Keynes asked cheerfully, picking up a car vacuum-cleaner from the bench. He snapped it open, withdrew the bag, and held out the bag to Gently.

Gently eyed him, then took the bag. It contained fluff, dust, sand and a glass bead. Gently wet his finger and dipped it in the dust: black mud, with no hint of red.

Keynes was watching him, his eyes for once serious.

'You see, I know what you don't yet know,' he said. 'This car wasn't used for the purpose you're thinking of, and neither was mine. What a shame we can't prove it.'

6

Gently ushered Keynes into the house, where Metfield had continued to maintain the presence. Maryon Britton jumped up nervily and hastened to grab Keynes by the arm.

'Oh, Edwin! I'm so glad you've got here.'

Keynes glimmered a smile at her. 'Steady on, Maryon.'

'You don't know. This man is terrible. He has just about accused me of murdering Adrian.'

'That's his job, my dear. He probably doesn't believe it.'

'But he *does*, Edwin. He *really* believes it. And there's nothing I can say to defend myself—he won't have it that I simply spent the night here with you!'

'Then we'll have to prove it to him,' Keynes said.

'But we *can't*, Edwin! How can we?'

'Oh, there'll be a way,' Keynes smiled confidently. 'It's what really happened, so it shouldn't be impossible.'

He sat himself easily on the long sofa, and Maryon Britton dumped herself beside him. Jennifer Britton had been wandering restlessly about the far end of the room. Now she came back to stand by the sofa. She stared at Keynes.

'Where's Lawrence?' she said.

Keynes ducked his head. 'Fiddling with a painting.

The water-meadows one, you remember? He'll be along later on.'

Jennifer Britton sniffed and took her place on the sofa. 'Lawrence is never around when he's wanted,' she said. 'And soon the Superintendent is going to ask me about my movements. Because if Mother didn't do it, it was probably me.' She flashed a defiant look at Gently.

'You didn't, did you?' Keynes said.

'Well, I might have done,' Jennifer Britton said. 'I was out in that direction that evening, and I can't even claim I was sleeping with someone. So I'm a dead duck, when he gets round to me. I can't think why Mother is going off the deep end.'

'Oh, be quiet, be quiet!' Maryon Britton snapped irritably. 'You're just a silly little goose, and that's plain to everyone.'

'I think the Superintendent likes me, rather,' Keynes said smoothly. 'So let's give him a chance, now, to put me through the mill.' He hooked the coffee-table towards him with his feet, re-lit his pipe, and dropped the match into a Venetian glass ashtray. 'Shoot,' he said to Gently. 'I'm longing to know how an expert goes about it.'

Gently folded his arms on the back of his chair, which he had reversed for greater comfort. He returned Keynes's gaze mildly. 'First, you can tell me about Mogi's Belt.'

Keynes's eyes twinkled through an issue of smoke. 'I rather set that up for you, didn't I?' he said. 'Well, it wasn't worth my while to conceal it. After all, I have lived in this area for ten years.'

'And you are familiar with that place?'

Keynes nodded. 'With all the district round about. I know the Battle Area as well as the military, and I never did step on a bomb yet. I discovered Mogi's

Belt years ago, before the lock on the gate got con-
veniently broken. And I can guess well enough what
Adrian was doing there. Though I'm hanged if I can
guess how *he* knew about it.'

'He could, of course, have been told,' Gently said.

'Only not by me,' Keynes grinned. 'I wouldn't have
told him, out of principle—I think badgers should
have their privacy respected. But he was told by
someone, that's pretty plain. He would never have
discovered it for himself. Adrian wasn't the type to
go vaguely rambling, to see what the fates had to
offer. As far as I know, his only other safari into the
forest was to photograph deer, and that was arranged
for him by Larling, the ranger—whom I imagine you
will have questioned.'

He paused. Gently said nothing.

'No,' Keynes said. 'So he didn't get it from Larling.
Unlikely anyway, since the Forestry are very properly jealous about things like badger setts. Which
leaves it something of a mystery. Outside the Forestry,
there can be very few people who know of the sett—
and none, I would have thought, who had it in for
Adrian. Which I take it is the theory you have in
mind.'

'You seem familiar with the Forestry,' Gently said.

'You can't live here and not be,' Keynes agreed.

'I understand they publish some excellent litera-
ture.'

Keynes let smoke trickle from his nostrils. 'Are you
referring to a certain Trail pamphlet?'

Gently hunched a shoulder, watching him.

'Yes, it's a possibility,' Keynes said. 'If one knew
that Adrian had such a pamphlet in his possession,
Did he?' His eyes held Gently's. 'I see. You must have
found one in the van. And it's not the sort of thing
one would have expected him to buy, so we assume
it was given by the murderer.' He nodded slowly. 'It

could have been enough. Adrian was never short of shrewdness. But once more, you're looking for a man with some small knowledge of Forestry matters.'

'About whom you can make no suggestion,' Gently said.

Keynes smiled. 'Nothing helpful.'

'A man so like you that he could be you?'

'I don't know such a man,' Keynes smiled.

'We did, of course, find a pamphlet,' Gently said. 'Exactly as your prescience suggests. It had been marked up for further guidance. Hand me that ball-pen from your pocket.'

Keynes hesitated, his smile thinning. Then he unclipped the pen and passed it over. Gently sketched a line with it across his palm. The colour of the ink was royal blue. He handed the pen back.

'Anything else?' Keynes asked.

'Yes. There was a latent fingerprint on the pamphlet. Have you any objection to us taking your fingerprints?'

Keynes's smile broadened again; he shook his head.

'Right, then,' Gently said. 'Perhaps now we can get to the real business. I want a full picture of what happened here on the evening of last Saturday. In fact, we'll begin a little earlier than that. You can give me your movements for the whole of Saturday. And it will help us both if you can give me also the names of some independent witnesses. Am I making it plain?'

'Too plain,' Keynes grimaced. 'Are you sure you shouldn't be giving us a caution?'

'Would you say that was necessary?'

Keynes rocked his shoulders. 'Just my big mouth,' he said. 'I'm easy meat for you.'

He knocked out his pipe humbly and sat back,

hands in the pockets of the jeans. Maryon Britton
sat stiffly; Jennifer Britton with her leg swinging.
From behind Gently, a faint rustle marked the turning of a page in Metfield's notebook.

'We'll begin with you, Mrs Britton.'

Maryon Britton gazed at him stonily. 'I've made one
statement already,' she said. 'I don't see why I should
have to make another.'

'Starting with Saturday morning,' Gently said.

Maryon Britton pouted. 'I had my bath. Breakfast.
Mrs Nixon arrived. I took the car into the village,
shopping. To the butcher's, the baker's and Hens-
man's Stores, all of whom will remember me. Back
to cook lunch. Eating lunch. Paying Mrs Nixon.
Reading in the garden. Jenny was playing tennis at
the sports ground: when she came in we had tea. Then
we watched TV for a while, and after that Edwin
came.'

'Did you make any phone calls?' Gently asked.

'One to Edwin at lunchtime.'

'Did you receive any?'

'No. And the only letters were bills.'

Gently nodded. 'Mr. Keynes?'

'I had a bath, too,' Keynes grinned. 'Also breakfast.
But I'm afraid the rest of my day was not quite so
well documented. I was writing reviews for the best
part of it, which is a sad thing to be doing on a Saturday. Then I switched on the box and caught a bit of
the second Test. Lawrence was with me in the morning—at least, he was working in his studio. But after
lunch he was at tennis, with Jenny. So I could have
been up to all kinds of devilment.'

'Was your car in use?'

'Not till the evening. Lawrence walked down to the
sports ground.'

'Did you make any phone calls?'

'I rang Television Centre, to ask Ivan Webster if Adrian was coming down.'

Gently hesitated. 'Then you know Ivan Webster?'

Keynes ghosted a shrug. 'Only in passing. He's been down here with Adrian a few times. I knew they were working together just then.'

'You spoke to him?'

'Yes.'

'What did he tell you?'

'He told me that Adrian wasn't happy with the script. Said they'd likely be working late. He didn't know if Adrian was planning to come down.' He paused. 'I couldn't very well ask him to ask Adrian. Adrian would have guessed who was wanting to know.'

'And why did you want to know?'

Keynes glanced at Maryon Britton.

'Oh, he's had it out of me,' she said huffily. 'Adrian was bringing down the will with him to burn in front of us. That's it in the briefcase.'

Keynes jingled some change in his pocket. 'There you have it, then,' he said. 'Lots of motive. You have just to decide if we're the sort of people who would kill for money. And naturally, we were wanting to know when the volcano would erupt, which was my reason for ringing Webster.'

'Mrs Britton suggested it, when she rang you at lunchtime?'

Keynes shook his head. 'My call was prior.'

'Did you mention the reason for your inquiry to Webster?'

'I did not. I scarcely know him.'

Gently paused. 'Then wouldn't it have seemed odd to him that you applied to him and not directly to Stoll?'

Keynes's eyes were thoughtful for a moment. 'Yes,

you'd have supposed so. But in fact he behaved as though my inquiry was quite natural.'

'As though, perhaps, he knew the reason for it.'

Keynes nodded. 'Interesting, isn't it? But of course, he's a pal of Nina Walling's, and she would've had the news from Adrian.'

Gently grunted. 'Getting back to your movements. Can anyone place you at your cottage during the day?'

'There's Fred Bishop. He's the milkman. He called to be paid, at about ten-thirty.'

'Nobody else?'

'No.'

'In the afternoon?'

'No.'

'So you can prove nothing about your movements.'

'Not a thing.' Keynes grinned. 'I'm the man you should really be going after.'

His flecked eyes rested on Gently's, smiling, alert, poised. Mrs Britton was also watching Gently, but her handsome eyes were anxious. As she watched, her hands drew together, and a little white showed at the knuckles.

Jennifer Britton's leg swung impatiently.

'Don't I get into this act?' she demanded. 'After all, I'm an unstable teenager, and thoroughly subversive. I could easily have done it.'

'You foolish girl!' her mother burst out. 'Don't you know better than to talk like that?'

Jennifer Britton tossed her ash-blonde locks and gazed expressively at the ceiling.

'Very well,' Gently said. 'Now we'll hear from you.'

'Oh, how kind,' Jennifer Britton said. 'I took the car into Latchford before Mother had it, and, inter alia, bought some things at Leeks.'

'Leeks . . . ?'

Metfield cleared his throat. 'They're the local ironmongers, sir. Gardening requisites and the like. Also agents for a certain product.'

'Gas,' Jennifer Britton said promptly. 'Bottles and bottles of glorious gas. A department that handles nothing else. Where we bought it during the power cut. And hoses too, all sorts of hoses—they're sure to stock the brand you want. And I was there on Saturday morning, which that nice young assistant will certainly remember.'

'You idiot!' her mother hissed. 'You went to buy some secateurs, and you know it.'

'Shush, Maryon,' Keynes smiled. 'Let Jenny tell her story in her own inimitable way.'

'Did you buy secateurs?' Gently asked.

'That was just my cover-up,' Jennifer Britton said. 'And there was nothing to stop me from buying gas and a yard or two of hose as well. In fact, I could have dropped it off at Mogi's whatsit, all ready for Adrian later on. No reason why not. Adrian could have told me he was camping there that night.'

'We could, indeed, assume that,' Gently said gravely.

Jennifer Britton glanced at him with narrowed eyes. 'So why don't you?' she said.

'I'll consider it, Miss Britton. But first, I'd like you to continue your statement.'

Jennifer Britton gave a snatch with her head. 'The rest of it isn't worth having,' she said. 'All goody-goody. I went around with Mother and was seen in exactly the same places as she was. Then after lunch I went to tennis, where we had a tournament with Latchford "A". About sixty witnesses, or thereabouts. And so home to tea and the box.'

'Did you drive to tennis?'

'Actually, no. The sports field is two hundred yards down the road.'

'Did you win the tournament?'

Jennifer Britton checked; then cuttingly rolled her eyes to the ceiling again.

'Thank you,' Gently said. 'Now we'll deal with the evening.' He turned to Keynes, who sat beaming at him. 'You first. I want a statement in detail, from the time you left your cottage until you returned there.'

Keynes eased back a peg on the sofa, his beam fading to an appealing smile.

'In detail,' he said. 'That's asking a bit much. But I'll do the best I can for you.' He wrinkled his brow. 'Lawrence came in at five—and to answer your question, they'd won the tournament. So then we had tea, which was a mixed grill, and tidied up, and came round here. Time, I should think, around seven; but I had no particular reason to notice.'

'When was the visit arranged?'

'Well—it wasn't, really. We spend most of our evenings together. And that evening we were anticipating Adrian, so our coming here was taken as read.'

'Any further phone calls?'

'None.'

'Did you walk or drive?'

'We drove.'

'So like that there were two cars here at the Grange.'

Keynes looked at him, and slowly nodded.

'Go on,' Gently said.

'Well, I parked in the yard, then we joined the ladies in here. We talked for a bit about the Adrian business and whether he really meant to chuck Maryon out. Honestly, I thought he would have cooled off it, because the strength of his affair with Nina was obvious. She was playing him along, and he must have known that, with all his shrewdness and experience of starlets. And meanwhile, Maryon was an excellent housekeeper. She could always be relied on to entertain his guests. So why chuck her out? I still think he wouldn't have done it, even though he meant to change his will.'

'Thank you, Edwin,' Maryon Britton said. 'I'm sure you were wrong—but thanks, anyway.'

'And you three and Lawrence Turner were all present,' Gently said.

'Oh yes, but not for long,' Jennifer Britton said. 'Lawrence was bored by it, and so was I. We went for a stroll—in the forest, of course.'

'When?'

'Oh . . . pretty soon.'

'At about half-past seven,' Keynes said.

'When did you return?'

'Who knows?' She shrugged.

'Getting dusk,' Keynes said. 'Around ten.'

Gently nodded. 'Then you and Mrs Britton were alone here from roughly half-past seven till ten. You had been discussing what Stoll intended. What else happened during that time?'

'Nothing,' Maryon Britton said bitterly. 'We were waiting for him—don't you understand? Waiting for Adrian. Just like characters in some beastly play by Becket.'

'That's about it,' Keynes agreed. 'When you're waiting, nothing ever happens but waiting. You talk and pour a drink and perhaps watch the box, but all you're really doing is waiting.'

'You never left this room?'

'Maryon made some coffee. I went through to the kitchen with her. We talked of holiday plans for a while, but the conversation always came back to Adrian.'

'You had no visitors?'

'None.'

'Phone calls?'

'None again.'

'And you made none—say, when it got late, when

you might have started wondering what had happened to Mr Stoll?'

Keynes shook his head. 'We didn't do much wondering, because we didn't know for sure if Adrian was coming. He'd left us to sweat, and we were doing it. He might easily have put off coming till the next weekend.'

'Webster told you he might be working late. It would have been a natural thing to put through a call to TV Centre.'

'We just weren't in the mood,' Keynes said. 'We didn't want to know—he would either come or he wouldn't.'

'And what's more,' Maryon Britton said, 'I wouldn't have wanted to give him the satisfaction of us inquiring after him.'

Gently shrugged massively. 'So you didn't inquire,' he said. 'You just passed the time talking and making coffee. But at some point you must have decided that Mr Stoll wasn't coming, and that his cousin could safely spend the night here. When was that?'

'Well . . . when it got later,' Maryon Britton said edgily.

'But how late?'

'I don't know! Naturally, when it got later, we stopped expecting him.'

'For example, you had never known him to arrive here late when his work had detained him in town?'

'Well—yes,' she said. 'It happened once or twice. But it wasn't something he made a habit of.'

'So why were you so certain on this occasion?'

'I wasn't certain! We took a chance.'

'It was me who was certain,' Jennifer Britton said tonelessly. '*I* told them that Adrian wasn't coming.'

'Oh, be quiet, be quiet!' Mrs Britton wailed.

'Why?' Jennifer Britton said. 'We want the truth,

don't we?' She gave a hysterical little laugh. 'You'd better ask me,' she said to Gently.

Gently considered her for a moment. She still sat relaxedly, her leg swinging. But there was a flush on her thin cheek, and her eyes were large and febrile. She was avoiding his gaze, looking beyond him: she was quivering slightly under his scrutiny.

'Very well,' he said. 'Tell me the truth, Miss Britton. How did *you* spend that evening?'

'Oh, of course, you'll be questioning Lawrence,' she said. 'So I couldn't tell you a fib, could I?'

'All your accounts will be checked.'

'Yes, and Lawrence is such a ninny. Though it would be his word against mine, wouldn't it? You would have to make your choice about that.' She smiled strangely. 'He wants to marry me,' she said. 'But that's neither here nor there. We went up through Taylor's Spinney, as far as the river, and sat on the grass by the bridge.'

'Which bridge is that?'

'Oh, just a bridge. But there's a telephone box right beside it. Not that I rang Adrian, or anything like that . . . but I could have done, couldn't I?'

'Did you?'

'You can ask Lawrence.'

'Of course she didn't!' Mrs Britton snapped. 'She's a stupid little girl, trying to make a mystery, and no idea how serious it is.'

'But I *could* have phoned Adrian . . . or anyone else.'

'Oh, I could shake you!' Mrs Britton cried. 'Superintendent, you had better ask Lawrence the truth of it. At least *he* has some common sense.'

Jennifer Britton smiled at nothing. 'I didn't ring him,' she said. 'I'd no need to. Because I knew—I'd known all day—that Adrian was never coming back to us.'

'How *could* you have known?' her mother stormed.

'I just sometimes know things,' Jennifer Britton said. 'And I knew this. A sort of echoey sadness. I told you about it when I came in.' She glanced at Keynes. '*You* remember.'

Keynes chuckled. 'Yes, I do. But I don't think it impressed us very much, Jenny. It was after you went to bed that we decided he wasn't coming.'

'But you do remember?'

He nodded.

'It was real, quite real,' Jennifer Britton said. 'All day, whenever I looked at something of Adrian's, I felt this queer sadness, so that I wanted to cry. And then, in the evening, I understood it—he wasn't coming back, then or ever.'

'Oh, what nonsense!' her mother cried.

'So I didn't ring anyone,' Jennifer Britton said. 'It was all going to happen, and *I knew it was*. Though I didn't actually know how or where.'

'Are you going to believe this?' demanded Maryon Britton of Gently.

Gently shrugged. 'Miss Britton seems very definite. But perhaps we should pass second sight for the moment, and return to the bare facts of her statement.'

Jennifer Britton flushed deeply. 'All right,' she said. 'Lawrence was horrid. He didn't understand me at all that evening. I shan't marry him, and that's that.'

'How long were you beside the bridge?'

'I don't know.'

'Did you see anyone there?'

'A stupid angler. But he was down the bank, among the rushes, and getting eaten alive by swarms of midges.'

'Did you meet anyone at all who would have known you?'

'No. Because we were keeping away from people.

We came back by Grimshoe Loke and the forest, and
we didn't meet anybody at all.'

'By the forest . . . ?'

Jennifer Britton made a face, and returned to her
meditation of the ceiling.

Gently nodded his mandarin nod. 'So now we've
followed it through to ten-thirty. No telephone calls,
no visitors, and only some premonitions about Mr
Stoll. Miss Britton has returned with her friend. There
is a car in the yard, and one in the garage. By now,
all this waiting would appear to be over, and dispositions for the night about to begin.' He looked at
Keynes.

'Just so,' Keynes smiled. 'About then we had given
Adrian up. And the circumstance seemed to confirm
my theory that my cousin was having second thoughts.'

'So the party began to break up.'

'Yes, sort of. Jenny was having a little fight with
Lawrence. Maryon was taking them both to task. So
Lawrence decided to shove off.'

'Taking your car?'

Keynes shook his head. 'The cottage is less than
a mile away. So the cars remained where they were—
though one was enough, for your theory.'

Gently grunted. 'And then?'

'I went to bed, too,' Jennifer Britton intoned. 'In
my own little room. Close to the backstairs. At the
other end of the house from Mamma's.'

'Thank you,' Gently said. 'And then?'

'We sat a while longer,' Keynes said. 'Till half-past
eleven, I suspect—just giving Adrian a last chance. I
suppose we were both thinking he might come very
late, intending to catch us *in flagrante delicto*; but as
it got towards midnight that possibility seemed to re-
cede. So we decided I would stay. I went outside to
lock my car—it was still there—then I locked up the

house for Maryon, and we retired. End of statement.'

'You wish it to end there?'

Keynes hesitated, his eyes quizzing Gently's. 'I'm afraid it will have to. I'm not taking it any further than the bedroom door.'

'I want a complete statement,' Gently said, 'going through till you returned to your cottage the next day. With special reference to the hours between midnight and three a.m.'

They stared at each other. There was still a smile latent on Keynes's lips, but his eyes were flat and steady, meeting Gently's without yielding. But the confrontation, if such it was, was ended by a sudden exclamation from Metfield, who jumped hastily to his feet and charged across to the French windows.

'This way, sir!'

He dived through them, landing in a skid on the gravel outside. When Gently arrived at the French windows, Metfield was sliding to a stop at the far end of the sweep.

'The other way, sir—cut him off!'

Gently turned to race along the front of the house. He cut round the corner, scattering gravel, and sprinted on towards the yard. A figure came flying out of the yard, saw Gently, halted, seemed about to come on; then Metfield flailed into view and hurled himself on the figure in a crunching tackle.

'Not this time, sonny!'

The man, a youngster, lay white-faced and gasping on the gravel. He was tallish and sported a full beard, and was wearing a green shirt with a tear in the sleeve.

7

'Get up,' Gently said.

For some moments the young man made no effort to obey him. Metfield, clearly a rugby type, had put all his beef into that tackle. Now his victim lay hugging his stomach and snatching air in gulped breaths. At last he climbed shakily to his feet.

'Are you Lawrence Turner?'

'That's me.'

'What were you running away from just now?'

'I—I wasn't running away. I just didn't want to—want to intrude.'

Metfield laughed scornfully. 'That's a good one! I spotted him listening outside the French windows.'

'No—I wasn't listening!'

'I'll bet he's been here all the time,' Metfield scoffed.

The young man kept panting and massaging his stomach. But then Jennifer Britton appeared at the door. She came forward quickly, her eyes flashing, and stood glaring at the policemen like an aroused Alsatian.

'What *on earth* have you been doing to Lawrence!'

'Just rounding him up, miss,' Metfield said.

'You haven't! You've been knocking him about. This is another sickening example of police brutality.'

'He was being elusive, miss. We had to collar him.'

'Look—you've done him some serious injury!'

'He's just winded, miss, that's all!' exclaimed Metfield, goadedly.

'Oh! You're worse than the thugs you're supposed
to protect us from.'

She moved protectively towards Turner, who was
beginning to regain control of his breathing. She laid
her hand on his arm and stared up into his still-
glazed eyes.

'Are you all right, Lawrence? What did they do to
you?'

'It's nothing—nothing,' he said huskily.

'If they knocked you about we can sue them, you
know.'

Turner swallowed and shook his head.

Now Maryon Britton and Keynes came out of the
house. Maryon Britton was looking grim. Keynes
sauntered easily towards the group; he slid Turner a
quick, compassionate grin.

'Time to be bold, Lawrence,' he said.

'Did he come here with you this afternoon?' Gently
asked.

Keynes shrugged and gestured with his hand. 'Not
much point in denying it, is there?' he said.

'So why didn't he come in with you?'

Keynes faded-in a smile. 'Every man has his reasons.
I'm sure that Lawrence's are quite innocent. Though
they may not therefore be wise. Shall we go inside?'

'No,' Gently said.

'No?'

'Turner will be accompanying me to the police
station.'

'Oh, but you can't do that!' Jennifer Britton burst
out.

'He will be assisting me there with my inquiries.'

They stared at him—Jennifer Britton angrily, her
mother stonily, Keynes with his smile.

'Perhaps I may have a few words with him first,'

Keynes said quietly. 'It could help you as well as him.'

'No.'

'Just as his adviser. He's only a kid of twenty-two, you know.'

Gently shook his head. 'If he needs an adviser he will be entitled to call one from the police station.' He looked from one to another of them. 'I shall want you there as well, to sign amendments to your previous statements. And I shall need possession of Mr Keynes's car in order to give it a thorough examination.'

There was a moment's silence.

'But this—this is so *unbelievable*!' Jennifer Britton cried.

'You may be making a bad mistake,' Keynes said earnestly.

Maryon Britton looked, but said nothing.

They left the Lodge in a small convoy, headed by Metfield, who was driving the Imp; then followed the Rapier, driven by Keynes, and finally the Wolseley, with Turner sitting beside Gently.

Turner had kept his mouth buttoned after that first, brief exchange, and he was keeping it buttoned now, his thin lips compressed and pale. He was a good-looking young man, as far as his looks got past his beard: a tall, though rather narrow, forehead, handsome dark eyes, and a nose of character. His hair and beard were golden brown, and he had a lean, athletic body. His hands, now clasping his sprawled knees, were large, with strong, big-boned fingers. He stared straight ahead throughout the drive, but with empty eyes that were seeing nothing.

At Latchford police station a reporter and his cameraman were mysteriously lurking on the steps. Metfield drove past them, into the M/T yard, but they were alert for Keynes and the two women. Then it was Gently's turn. He pulled out round the Rapier and swept into the yard after Metfield, but the camera caught them, with Turner's hands going up in a foolish attempt to cover his face. Gently slammed to a stop.

'Do you want press attention?'

Turner shivered. 'Please . . . no!'

Gently grunted. 'Well you've got it now! If we don't crucify you, they will.'

He hustled Turner through the back door and shoved him into an interrogation-room. Then he hurried through reception, where the other three were waiting, and out again to the steps. The reporter blocked his way directly.

'Chiefie—tell us! Is it a pinch?'

'No it isn't! Just public-minded citizens giving the police a little assistance.'

'That was Maryon Britton and her daughter.'

'Are you asking me or telling me?'

'Who was beardie?'

'He's an Irish gentleman who thought you were going to take a pot at him.'

'Now, Chiefie, give us a break! He's helping with your inquiries, isn't he?'

'Everyone is helping with my inquiries, with the small exception of two present.'

The reporter's pencil scuffled over his notebook.

'Chiefie, give us a name, can't you? We know the other man, Stoll's cousin, but the lad with the beard is a new face.'

'If he's got something for us I'll tell you later.'

'Chiefie, that's as much as to say it's a pinch.'

'So print it and listen for the bang.'

'Now, Chiefie! Don't you trust us?'

Gently turned back into the station. He met Metfield coming in from the M/T yard. The local man was rubbing his hands and he had a glint in his eye.

'Where's chummie?'

'In the sweat-room. You'd better put a man in there with him. That reporter has snouted him already. He'll be stop-press in the late editions.'

'Do we take him now?'

Gently shook his head vigorously. 'Let's get those amendments down and signed. Then we can move in on chummie. He seems the sort who could sweat tender.'

Metfield took a joyous swallow of his tongue. 'He's our boyo, sir!' he said. 'It came out plain when you were interrogating. Turner is where it all points to.'

'Maybe,' Gently grunted.

'Yes sir, it stops with him,' Metfield gloated. 'The others are in it, I'll swear to that, but Turner was the one who turned the gas on.' He took another happy swallow. 'Because look, sir, Turner is the one without an alibi. And he was planning to marry the daughter, to cut himself in on the deal. Keynes is maybe the brains, the man with the know-how to set it up—but it was Turner who came back for the car and drove into the forest with the gas. And we'll break him, sir, that's certain, and he'll put a finger on the others. We just have to play it right—we can have it licked by this time tomorrow!'

Gently stared woodenly at the local man. 'Did you ever buy a bottle of gas?' he asked.

'Me?' Metfield's eyes rounded. 'No sir, I never did.'

'It works like this,' Gently said. 'You pay a fiver for the bottle, and an odd sum for the gas. After that you just pay for the gas, exchanging your bottle for one of theirs. Then, if you've finished with using gas, you can get a refund on the bottle, less a percentage for deterioration calculated from the date of the original purchase. Can you get two search warrants in a hurry?'

Metfield gulped. 'Yes, sir!'

'Right. I think it's time we used them—one for the Lodge, one for Keynes's cottage.'

'B-but are we looking for something special, sir?'

Gently's brows lifted. 'There is of course a contract with every bottle. The retailer enters the date of purchase. We may just be dealing with a careless chummie.'

Metfield reddened. 'I should have known about that, sir. But the agent I spoke to didn't mention it.'

Gently hunched. 'Probably a long shot.'

Metfield bustled away to his office.

It was early in the evening before they got round to Turner. Low sun was shining dazzlingly through the interrogation-room window. Turner was sitting forlornly at the bare, scrubbed table, which, with three chairs, was the only furniture in the room. But there were paper and pencils on the table, for the better accommodation of cooperative chummies, and during his hours of waiting Turner had made some use of these. He had drawn the two constables who had taken turns at sitting with him. He had drawn the plastic tray on which they had brought him tea and sandwiches. Then he had drawn a memory sketch of, it appeared, the dell in Mogi's Belt; but now he was just sitting, with his head resting on his hands.

He didn't look up when Gently entered with Metfield. Metfield nodded to the constable, who left. The room was stuffy and smelled of floor polish: was unnaturally irradiated by the flashing sun.

'Lawrence Turner?'

Turner drew a deep sigh and straightened up in his chair. His face was flushed, but that was probably due to the close atmosphere of the room. He looked dully at Gently.

'Stand up, Turner. Turn out your pockets on the table.'

Turner hesitated, then obeyed; making two small heaps, one from each pocket. In one heap was a pipe, matches, a packet of twist tobacco, a penknife; in the other money, a dogeared notebook, a stub of pencil, and a ring with two keys. Gently fingered the latter. One was a Union door-key. The other was embossed: Rootes.

'The key of Mr Keynes's car?'

Turner nodded, saying nothing. Gently picked up the notebook. It contained sketches, quotations and a few naïve verses. The money amounted to little over a pound. The penknife was a cheap smoker's knife. The pipe was a charred corncob, which had probably cost forty pence.

'Do you want a smoke?'

'Yes—please.'

'Where did you tear the sleeve of your shirt?'

Turner dropped his eyes. 'Well—it was yesterday—I tore it on a nail.'

Gently took out the envelope containing the fibres he had removed from the gate at Mogi's Belt. He went round to Turner. He took out the fibres. Plainly they came from the sleeve of the shirt.

'All right. You can smoke now.'

Turner sagged in the chair again. His hands fumbled with the twist and the penknife, but they were like the hands of a blind man. Gently pulled up a chair, across the table from him. Metfield settled at the end of the table; he laid his notebook open before him, and sharpened a pencil with firm strokes. At last, Turner had his pipe going. Gently leaned towards him over the table.

'Now. What makes you so interested in our business?'

Turner puffed nervously at the corncob. 'I-I'm not interested. It's how I told you. I didn't want to intrude till you were gone.'

'And this morning?'

'I-I was in Latchford.'

Gently shook his head. 'That's not where your shirt was. And there's a lot of red dust on Mr Keynes's car. Not the sort of dust you find in Latchford.'

'But that could have been picked up at any time!'

'Like the red stain on the tyres?'

'W-what red stain?'

'The sort of stain you pick up on the track by Mogi's Belt, after rain.'

Turner puffed furiously. 'I don't know about that! And I've never driven a car round there. I've told you why I didn't come in with Edwin, and I don't have to say any more.'

Gently leaned back from the table. 'Listen,' he said. 'You were at Mogi's Belt this morning. You were spying to see what we were up to, and when you were spotted you ran away. Then this afternoon you drove to the Lodge with Mr Keynes and you saw a police car parked in the yard. Mr Keynes came in, but you didn't. You hung about outside, trying to eavesdrop. That's twice in one day you've played that trick, and twice you've tried to give us the slip. And you're the driver of a car that was at Mogi's Belt at about the time Mr Stoll was killed. Of course you don't have to say any more—and you'll know best whether to keep your mouth shut. But either you talk, or we shall have to assume that there are very good reasons for your silence. So the ball is in your court. It's up to you how you play it.'

The pipe was trembling in Turner's fingers. 'Are—are you arresting me?' he faltered.

Gently folded his arms comfortably and gazed at the wall above Turner's head.

'Look,' Turner said. 'Look—I'm innocent! I didn't kill Mr Stoll. I know it looks bad, but I didn't do it—please! You've got to give me a chance.'

Gently shrugged at the wall. 'Somebody did kill him.'

'I know—I know—but it wasn't me! I was in bed—I went straight home. I don't know anything about it at all!'

'Then why were you spying and trying to avoid us?'

'Because—because—!' Turner stuttered. 'I knew you'd be after me, don't you see? I had to find out what you were up to.'

Gently grunted contemptuously. 'How likely!'

'But it's the truth!' Turner exclaimed.

'I could believe that someone else put you up to it.'

'No—no! It was because of myself.'

'And why were we going to bother with you?'

Turner brought hand and pipe down on the table. 'Because I was alone. I couldn't prove anything. It was just my word—my word only!'

And suddenly his flush had turned to pallor, and his eyes were beginning to stare. He lolled sideways, pushing heavily on the table; sweatbeads were showing on his blanched forehead.

Gently got up hurriedly and shoved open the door. 'Fetch a glass of water!' he bawled to the constable. Then he went to wrestle with the paint-sealed window.

Behind him, Turner was vomiting over the table.

So now the room was stinking of Jeypine, but at least the window was ajar. Also, Gently had drawn one of the blue cotton curtains to cut out the buzzing glare.

Turner, cleaned up and hugging a glass, looked damp and fragile amongst his beard. His dark eyes were large and vacant and he sat slumped, one arm supporting him.

The picture of a killer? Gently shrugged to himself. The young painter had crumpled like wet paper.

'How well did you know Stoll?'

Turner hugged the glass a little closer. 'I saw him often, of course . . . I've been living at the cottage for a year.'

'Like him?'

Turner was silent for a space. 'I . . . admired what he did. He was an artist, a true artist. There was no getting away from that.'

'But did you like him?'

Turner wrestled with the glass. 'He wasn't . . . he was different from other men. He had this gift, this great gift. It somehow . . . swamped him. You had to accept that.'

'You found him inhuman.'

'In a way—yes!'

'Egotistic and calculating.'

'Well . . . yes . . .'

'Other people didn't count. He just drove them.'

'I suppose so . . . it seemed like that.'

'So he was asking for what he got.'

'No!' Turner raised his eyes to Gently's. 'It wasn't like that. You couldn't really hate him. Because you felt he couldn't help himself, either.'

'That's a charitable viewpoint.'

'But it's true. Everyone had that feeling about Adrian. He had this talent which he had to live with, and it didn't give him room to be like other people. He had to be a dictator. That was his job. He could only work by imposing his will. Every creator must be a dictator, but Adrian's material was human beings. So in a way, he had to keep acting like God, and if he lost the touch he couldn't do his job.'

'You would have thought it was something he could have left in town.'

Turner shook his head. 'I think he tried. But he couldn't really let up, ever. Just as I can't let up seeing things as pictures.'

'So you admired him though you didn't like him.'

'I think . . . perhaps, I liked him too.'

'Did he buy your pictures?'

'No, he didn't. But once he invited me to stay in town.'

'What was that about?'

Turner shuffled the glass. 'I think just that he thought it would do me good. You know, meet people, get in the swim. There's nothing of that sort doing out here.'

'And did you meet people? For example, Nina Walling?'

Turner coloured faintly. 'Yes, I met her. But I had met her and Ivan Webster before, when Adrian brought them down to the Lodge.'

'Friends of yours.'

'No—never!' He jerked the glass, slopping some water. 'I don't think they were friends of Adrian's either, whatever was going on between them.'

Gently nodded. Turner gulped some water. Metfield's pencil scribbled, and was silent.

'You were at the Lodge last Sunday week?'

'Yes,' Turner said. 'I was there.'

'Was Mr Stoll very likeable on that occasion?'

Turner stared at the glass. 'They were all upset.'

'They?'

He shrugged weakly. 'It was nothing to do with me, was it?'

'I would have thought it had some connection.'

Turner studied the glass and said nothing.

'For example,' Gently said. 'Mr Stoll expressed intentions which would have been very detrimental to your friends. Detrimental to Mr Keynes. Detrimental to Miss Britton.'

Turner flushed. 'It was still none of my business . . . l'

'Aren't you informally engaged to Miss Britton?'

'I . . . no! There's nothing definite . . .'

'But you have proposed to her?'

'It . . . it's been mentioned.'

'Then in that case,' Gently said, 'you must have been deeply interested in Mr Stoll's intentions. Because they affected your future prospects equally with those of Miss Britton and her mother. They would also affect your immediate prospects as the protégé of Mr Keynes, who would no longer be able to rely on Mrs Britton when he was going through a bad patch. On the whole, you would be the most affected —because you are the one who is nearest the breadline.'

'I . . . I didn't *think* of it like that!'

Gently spread his hands wearily. 'You, of course, are the dedicated artist who never thinks about these things?'

'No, but——!'

'So you thought about it! Just like the others, you thought about it! And you came to the conclusion that the only answer to the problem lay in the removal of Mr Stoll.'

'But that's not *true*!' Turner banged the glass on the table.

'Not true that Mr Stoll's death would be the answer to your troubles?'

'Not true that I thought it . . . that I—!'

'Just when did you get the stain on those tyres?'

Turner stared at him, eyes wide, mouth contracted and in a droop. The glass was bobbing in his hand and threatening to decant its contents.

'You're trying to *make* me say things!'

'I want the truth.'

'No—you think I'm guilty now.'

'If you are not, you can explain to me. When did you get the stain on the tyres?'

Turner groaned and closed his eyes. Somehow he

got the glass back safely on the table. He drew his shaking hand away from it and passed the hand over his brow.

'On Sunday.'

'At what time?'

'It was the evening. After tea.'

Gently waited till Metfield's pencil ceased to flow across the page.

'Go on.'

'I was on my own . . . the police weren't interested in me then. But I knew . . . I thought I had better find out all I could about it. So I borrowed the car and went along there.'

'How did you know where to go?'

'We were up at the Lodge that afternoon. When the police told us. They mentioned the place. They seemed to think it could have been suicide.'

'And you knew the place they spoke of?'

'Yes. I'd been round there once with Edwin.'

'Who showed you the badger sett, of course?'

Turner hesitated, nodded. 'So I drove round there. And I met the police driving the cavarette towards town. So I thought it would be safe to carry on. There was nobody about when I got there.'

'What exactly did you hope to find?'

Turner stared at the glass for a moment. 'I don't know. Something—anything. I felt I just had to go and look.' He shuddered. 'I knew you would get round to me. You would have to start thinking the way you are thinking. Once you had checked up properly on the others I would stick out like a bent penny. So I had to do my best, to be ready for you, to find out everything I could. But it amounts to the same thing, doesn't it? You're going to have me in the end.'

'Perhaps,' Gently said. 'Is that a confession?'

'I didn't kill Adrian,' Turner said.

'Then your fingerprints couldn't be on the caravette.'

Turner shook his head. 'I've never been near it.'

'Nor on documents inside the caravette.'

Turner's eyes were uneasy. 'I don't see how they could be.'

'Say, on a map?'

He kept shaking his head.

'A certain pamphlet?'

Turner just looked blank.

'Right,' Gently said. 'So let's hear your version of how Mr Stoll discovered the badger sett. I'm sure you've been giving the matter some thought, at intervals of checking up on the police.'

Turner coloured again. He sipped water. 'Somebody must have told Adrian,' he said. 'Adrian wouldn't have gone looking for it himself. He had other people do his research for him.'

'Go on,' Gently said.

Turner licked his lips. 'Well . . . somebody who knows the forest pretty well.'

'Like Mr Keynes?'

'Yes . . . like that. Or one of the rangers . . . somebody.'

'Somebody,' Gently said. 'And when would they have told him?'

Turner jiffled with the glass. 'Well, probably during the week. Otherwise he'd have been filming the previous weekend. But he didn't bring his gear with him then.'

'Couldn't he have been told during that weekend?'

'I don't see how,' Turner said. 'Edwin and I were the only visitors, and the row began soon after we got there.'

'The row in which you took no part.'

Turner jerked the glass. 'Yes, I told you.'

'So that you, at any rate, finished up on speaking terms with Mr Stoll?'

Turner nursed the glass and said nothing.

'Yes,' Gently said. 'You had kept in the background. Mr Stoll wasn't aiming at you. He perhaps wasn't conscious that you were involved in the measures with which he was threatening the others. You, after all, were his great admirer. He had responded by inviting you to stay at his flat. It might even have been that he had some notion of taking his cousin's talented protégé. So you weren't in opposition during that row. You were neutral, or a silent ally. And later on, during the week, it was open to you to visit him, or at least to communicate in a friendly way. Isn't that so?'

'I didn't visit him!' Turner exclaimed.

'No phone call, followed by a letter with an enclosure?'

'No!'

'But there could have been,' Gently said. 'And that's the point, isn't it? There could have been.'

He sat back, studying Turner, who was crouched, and clutching the glass like a weapon. The young man's smoky dark eyes stared back at him with a fearful, baffled expression.

'Yes, there could have been,' Gently mused. 'And then it would all fit together. We could show how Mr Stoll came to be where he was, and how his killer knew he would be there. We could show motive, premeditation and opportunity, backed by evidence of presence at the spot, plus some knowledge of bottled gas derived from its use during emergency power cuts. Which, of course, is enough to be going on with while we complete our investigation.' He paused. 'Have you any comments?'

'I didn't do it. I *didn't!*'

'Didn't you return to the Lodge on the Saturday night and take Mr Keynes's car from the yard?'

'No!'

'You didn't pick up a gas bottle and a length of hose, and drive into the forest?'

'No!'

'You didn't kill Mr Stoll?'

'No!'

'Then,' Gently said, 'who did kill him?'

Turner was sitting up straight, his eyes wild, his hands clenched: now his mouth dropped open stupidly and his eyes seemed to lose focus.

'Not—not me!'

'So who?'

'I *don't know*!' Turner gabbled. 'Me—I'm the only one who could have, might have—you can't suspect any of the others.'

'Not Mr Keynes?'

'No!'

'Mrs Britton?'

'Oh, no!'

'That leaves Miss Britton.'

'Oh God, never! You couldn't believe that of Jenny.' He gasped for breath. 'Look, it wasn't us—you must *know* it wasn't us! We're people, civilized people, we'd never have dreamed of such a thing. Even me—I know I look guilty—you've got to think that I'm guilty— but even me—how can you really believe that I would kill Adrian?'

'Perhaps nobody killed him,' Gently grunted. 'Perhaps that's a dummy lying in the morgue.'

Turner banged his fist down. 'But it wasn't us! Why can't I get you to believe the truth? And if it wasn't us, it was nobody here—it must have been that gang up in town—they'd do it, too, I know they would —and that's where Adrian was all week!'

Gently gazed at him. 'What gang?'

'The Wallings—Webster—their hangers-on! They're callous, immoral. They'd do anything. That's where you should look—not down here.'

'Thank you,' Gently said. 'Now suggest their motive.'

'I don't *know* of any motive.'

Gently clicked his tongue. 'That's too bad! When your own motive sticks out a mile.'

'Look,' Turner exclaimed desperately. 'There's got to be one! If you ask around you're sure to find it—a motive big enough—bigger than mine—a motive!' He broke off, panting.

'Well?' Gently said.

Turner was staring unseeingly, his breath coming in suppressed gulps. His fingers crooked and uncrooked, the nails scraping the bare table-top. Then he shook his head idiotically.

'No—no good—you wouldn't swallow it! Not from me. But there has to be a motive—and you can find it—if you'll only look!'

'And that's all you're telling me?'

Turner's head bobbed slackly.

Gently sighed and rose from his chair. 'Then now we'll give the truth a little help. Inspector Metfield will take your dabs.'

Turner submitted to the process sullenly, then relapsed into his hunched slump over the table. They took the dabs card into Metfield's office and made the comparison with the dab on the Trail pamphlet. Another negative result—the others had been Keynes and the two Brittons. Which, of course, didn't prove that none of them had handled it: merely that if they had, there was no proof. The two searches, overseen by Metfield's sergeant, Shadwell, had been similarly unproductive.

Metfield regarded the evidence sourly.

'That's our clincher gone,' he said. 'But like you said, we've enough to go on with. I reckon it would stick with what we've got.'

Gently drew on his pipe; then shook his head.

'You don't reckon so?' Metfield said.

'No. It's only half a case yet. A good defence counsel would rip it to shreds. Also'—he idled smoke—'what was your impression of Turner?'

'Turner?' Metfield stared. 'I'd say he'll crack in twenty-four hours.'

Gently got up and went over to the window, where he stood puffing with his back to Metfield. The local man gazed after him apprehensively, at the solid figure with its heavy shoulders. Gently removed his pipe.

'Turn him loose.'

'Sir!' Metfield half-choked on his tongue.

'We don't have a case against him that will stand up, so we can't charge him. Turn him loose.'

'But—but—!' Metfield came to his feet, colour flooding his stubbly jowls. Gently turned mildly from the window to survey his disturbed colleague.

'Look! I don't think he did it, though someone may have used him to set it up. So I'd sooner he was running loose than being sick over issue tables.'

'But we can't just let him go, sir!'

Gently smiled silkily. 'Yes we can. We've given him a little touch of the plague, and now I want to see where he'll carry it.'

Metfield gulped. 'A touch of what plague, sir?'

'Fear,' Gently said. And resumed his pipe.

8

Over a cup of tea in bed the next morning, Gently reviewed that snap decision. Had he talked himself into it a little, in the way he had handled the Turner interrogation? He examined each stage of the questioning critically. No: he had reserved his judgement till the end. At no point had he allowed himself to treat Turner as any other than an urgent suspect. If the evidence of the fingerprints had been positive he would have accepted it and begun the marathon process of cracking Turner; it was not till then, till the prints failed to match, that he had permitted the judgement suddenly to click. So why now was he querying it, checking it through cautiously, wondering if he was quite so certain this morning?

Turner had received his release in silent stupor, as though unable to grasp what was being said to him. Gently had handed him over to Keynes, who had returned to wait for him after accompanying Sergeant Shadwell to the search of Deerview Cottage. If Keynes was surprised, he had concealed it. This was what he had been expecting, his smile seemed to say. Gently had had his turn with Turner, as with the others, and now they could all call it a day. A bit of obligatory routine . . . and of course, Gently would kindly release the car?

And Gently had released it, just like that, as though agreeably confirming the Keynes script: the car having been minutely scrutinized in the meantime, and samples taken from the tyres and underbody. The two of them had then driven away, using the rear access to avoid the reporters, with Turner sitting dazedly beside Keynes, and Keynes waving cheerily to Gently and Metfield.

A tactical mistake? Gently poured more tea from the Sun's generous plated teapot. No . . . in some way it was right. It fitted the style which the case was insensibly developing. The case needed rope, room to breathe . . . a decisive move at this point would be a mistake.

He checked his watch, then lifted the phone. After a few more sips he was through to Lyons. Lyons had been to Brighton the previous day and had returned convinced that Walling's alibi was faked.

'This Vivian Chance is a proper nana, sir. He's been done a couple of times for soliciting. One involved a kid under age. I doubt if counsel would risk calling him.'

'What's his story, then?'

'Nothing he can prove. He has a flat in a block facing the front. Separate entrance in a side-road. Lock-up garage at the rear.'

'Still, what's he saying?'

'Same tale as Walling, sir. That Walling was there when he says he was. Arrived Saturday lunchtime, left at seven-thirty on Sunday.'

'And didn't leave the flat all that time?'

'Yes, sir. They went for a drive on Sunday. Into Lewes then down to Eastbourne, and a picnic on the downs at Beachy Head.'

'But no witnesses.'

'None, sir. Unless they were spotted at Beachy Head. But it's pretty thick there on Sundays, and that was the only place where they're supposed to have stopped. I checked with the other residents in the block and with the occupant of the flat overlooking the garages. Then I hunted up Chance's milkman, to see if he'd ordered extra on Sunday.'

'And had he?'

'No, sir. The usual two pints.'

'That would do, if they skipped the cornflakes.'

'But it was his regular order for Sundays, sir,' Lyons said patiently. 'You'd have expected him to increase it, if he had a guest.'

Gently grunted. 'He could have forgotten! We still can't prove Walling wasn't in Brighton.'

'And he can't prove he was, sir,' Lyons said firmly. 'And that's all I'll need when I pull him in.'

Gently asked him about Webster. Lyons had put a D.C. on it. Webster's account of his movements tallied. His car, the Volvo, had been seen parked in its usual slot outside his flat, on Saturday evening. At about eleven p.m. he called at the Capri, and there had picked up Nina Walling. He had dropped her at Campden Hill soon after midnight, and then, presumably, had returned to Battersea. His car was seen parked there at six a.m.

'I'd say that wrapped him up, sir,' Lyons said. 'Messiter saw him when he dropped off Miss Walling. Theoretically, he could have got out there and done the job, but he would have to have driven like the clappers. And what would be his motive?'

Gently sipped tea. 'How much do we know about the people he mixes with?'

'Well—not a lot, sir. They'll be the usual sort of crowd—TV, theatre, and hangers-on.'

'Perhaps we ought to know more.'

He could sense Lyons's silent groan. 'You want me to chase it up for you, sir?'

Gently nodded to himself. 'Yes, chase it up. And especially any part of it that mixed with Stoll too.'

He hung up and finished his tea; then lifted the

phone and dialled again. This time it was Keynes's un-
hurried voice that reponded to the ring.

'Deerview Cottage. Edwin Keynes.'

'Chief Superintendent Gently,' Gently said.

'Oh . . . yes.' There was a brief, muffled period
when Keynes had certainly covered the mouthpiece.
Then he came back. 'Sorry—getting breakfast! Had
to switch off the kettle. What can I do for you?'

'I want a word with you. Let's say ten sharp this
morning.'

'Hold on, please.' Another muffled period, this time
longer than the first. 'Right—that's better! Ten is
fine. Shall I come to you, or will you come to me?'

'I'll come to you.'

'Then here's a suggestion. I like a stroll through
the trees after breakfast. Suppose you join me? We
can be quite private, and a stroll through the trees
clears the brain.'

Gently hesitated. 'Through Mogi's Belt?'

He heard Keynes chuckle. 'Not unless you want to!
I suggest you meet me at St Mary's church, which is
on the left before you reach the village. How's that?'

'Very well.'

'Fine,' Keynes said. 'I hate missing my walk. It's a
glorious day. If our talk disappoints you, you'll still
have the pleasure of breathing pure air.'

Gently laid down the phone slowly—had he just
let Keynes get away with something? A stroll in the
forest meant he wouldn't visit the cottage: wouldn't
encounter the vulnerable Turner. Was that the ob-
ject . . . protection of Turner, who by now might
be ready to sing a little louder? Well, it could be
circumvented simply enough by a prior visit to the
cottage . . .

Gently hunched a pyjama-clad shoulder. No, he
would go on playing it Keynes's way! Turner was

available; and if he was needing protection, then he'd be none the worse for extra stewing.

And meanwhile . . . a study of Keynes's tactics. Perhaps the forest *was* a good idea!

St Mary's church was a small flint building, at least a mile from West Brayling Village. It was reached by a short, sign-posted lane, departing from the road near where it left the forest. The church stood by the trees, and rather under them, since they overtopped its round Saxon tower; the little nave had thick-fluted Norman windows with dog-tooth carving, and a blue pantile roof. There was a massive and sunny quietness about it as it stood silently in its scythed churchyard, where the tombstones were patched with lichens and carved with the cherubs of earlier centuries.

Keynes was lounging at the wrought-iron gate as Gently glided the Lotus to a stop. He was chewing a stem of Timothy grass, and he ran an appreciative eye over the white car. He grinned as Gently got out.

'Your trade pays better than mine,' he said. 'If you know any villains who make films, put in a word for Edwin Keynes.'

Gently slammed the door and locked it. 'How much do you make in a year?' he asked.

Keynes's grin widened. 'About as much as a dustman. And they tell me I'm one of the lucky ones.'

'So you're short of money.'

Keynes laughed. 'Who isn't?' He chewed his stem, his eyes amused. 'But not currently. A fortnight ago I had an advance payment from America.'

'Which makes you about solvent.'

Keynes nodded. 'About. And much too indolent to murder for more.'

'Unlike someone who was here lately.'

Keynes chewed equably. 'Unlike someone.'

He met Gently's stare impishly. He was dressed in
a faded sports-shirt, jeans and sandals. He had a
tanned, sturdy, outdoors look, with a poised strength
in his lounging frame.

'Do I look like someone who needs money?'

'Like someone without it,' Gently said.

'But someone who needs it?'

Gently shrugged. 'When you have a purpose, then
you need it.'

'Right,' Keynes smiled. 'For a purpose you need it.
And really I have very little purpose. I use the lumps
that turn up travelling, and that's about the only
purpose I have. For the rest, I'm too rich to bother
with money. It's too expensive for me to earn. It
doesn't buy anything that I have a mind to. I'm a
millionaire without lifting a finger.' He chewed for
a moment. 'Look, compare the two of us. You must
earn at least twice as much as I do. You arrive at
this spot in an expensive car, and wearing a suit that
would take me to Athens. Yet, why have you come?
You've come out of duty, hoping to catch yourself a
murderer. And I have come because of the trees,
and the effect of sunlight on a wall. The pound in
your pocket won't buy you what I possess with my
pocket empty.'

'But it will pay the rent,' Gently said. 'And take
care of people we may be fond of.'

'Oh, granted,' Keynes laughed. 'Though that doesn't
need a fortune, either. But take my point. I'm a man
of some freedom. The money motive is too weak for
me. I might stray into unlawfulness by other paths,
but not this. It lacks credibility.'

'Then what would be credible for you?' Gently said.

Keynes shook his head, grinning. 'Let's walk,' he
said. 'We may stumble on the truth among the trees—
or enough for our mortal purpose.'

He tossed his stalk into the churchyard and set off

along the lane. Within a hundred yards it entered
the forest at a ride, numbered eighty-seven. The sections here were Corsican pine. The ride sloped down
gently to a green distance. As one approached, and
then entered the trees, the sweet smell of resin seemed
to expand one's lungs.

'My favourite stroll,' Keynes said, breathing deeply.
'Beginning and ending at the church. Walking before
work is a habit of years. Not that I'm writing a book
just now.'

'What are you doing?' Gently asked.

'Lazing and thinking,' Keynes grinned. 'I finished
a book two months ago—alas, you can't turn them out
like sausages. But now some money has come I'll away
to Scotland, which is the only place to go in summer.
Then, in the autumn, I'll beat my head, and trust
that inspiration will result.'

'Were you working last week?' Gently asked.

'Just reading review books,' Keynes said. 'Which
would give me plenty of time to plot Adrian's down-
fall—though none to persuade him to film badgers.' He
chuckled. 'I could perhaps help you. But you'll have
to think of intelligent questions.'

Gently was silent. They walked on through the
continuous cathedral of the trees. There was a beaten
track down the centre of the ride, and faint tracks of
a vehicle on the rough verges. All along the path fluttered Speckled Wood butterflies, seeking the sunned
patches of greyish sand; they rose irritably at the ap-
proach of footfalls, danced a few figures, then settled
again. Wildflowers were scant: a few white campions and yellow-green cushions of wild mignonette;
but brambles trailed confidently under the trees along
with colonies of fragile, over-tall nettles. Birds were
more plentiful. A variety of tits were hunting, mouse-
like, among the twigs. Tree-creepers shuffled around
the trunks, and now and then a wren popped up

flirtatiously. Then, from some distant glade, echoed the demented tatting of a woodpecker, oddly resonant: occasionally his mocking, uncanny cry.

'You'll see a deer here sometimes,' Keynes said. 'Though usually only the flash of his rump. And further on, in the Scots, there are plenty of red squirrel. I'll show you their drey when we come to it. We may just catch a glimpse of one in flight.'

Gently snorted. 'A strange place to kill a man!'

Keynes glanced at him sidelong. 'Yes. The plains and the deserts are the killing grounds. Here you have the moral influence of the trees.'

'The moral influence?'

Keynes nodded. 'Trees are a sort of dolphin of the vegetable world. They love men. If you can walk in a forest and not feel that love, you are past redemption.' He laughed suddenly. 'Don't take my word for it. Cast your mind back over history. The cruel and war-like people have lived in plains, the cruellest of all in the deserts. Men need trees. When they are de-prived of them they become decadent and savage. If we are to become like gods, and not like devils, it will be through the influence of trees.'

'But trees are insensate things,' Gently said.

Keynes shook his head. 'Never. When Wordsworth spoke of flowers enjoying the air they breathe he was half-way to the truth—in his simpering fashion. Trees, flowers, all the slow-livers, are as sensate as you or I. It is only our arrogance that makes us blind to it, and our power to dispose and destroy. If you wound a tree, it bleeds. If you injure it, it falls sick. And if you protect and encourage it, it shows its pleasure, and tries to respond by pleasing you. They live more slowly than we, but not differently, and perhaps are greater than us in love.'

'Well,' Gently shrugged.

Keynes chuckled. 'I see I'm talking too earnestly,'

he said. 'After all, we came here to discuss lesser matters, like whether you can believe I killed Adrian.
Are you any further with that yet?'

'Should I be?' Gently said.

'I'm clearly next on your list,' Keynes smiled.
'Since Lawrence was a cock that wouldn't fight.
What turned you against him, by the way?'

Gently said nothing. Keynes watched him smilingly.

'You must have had a fairish go at the lad,' he
said. 'Lawrence usually talks to me, but after his session with you he simply shut up shop. Didn't want to
tell me, didn't want to meet the others. He went off
on his own, then went to bed.' He paused. 'I even
got the impression that you had sold him the notion
that I was guilty.'

His eyes sought Gently's. Gently met them woodenly. 'He would be seeing the facts squarely,' he said.

'Only that isn't a fact,' Keynes said. 'And him seeing them squarely would show him it wasn't.' He
walked on some paces, then sighed. 'Never mind.
One is pretty resilient, at twenty-two. Lawrence was
more himself this morning. He took the day off and
went into town.'

Gently stopped dead. 'He did what?'

Keynes glanced surprise. 'Went into town. To London. He borrowed the car. I thought he needed a
break, after yesterday.'

'Was this before or after I rang you?'

'After.' Keynes grinned. 'Do you think he was
dodging you?'

'I think he was. And I think you suggested it.'

'Oh, come on, now!' Keynes smiled.

He plucked another stem of grass and began to
chew it unhurriedly, with a tickled expression.

'You want him out of the way,' Gently said. 'Either he knows something, or he's guessed it.'

'Of course, you would think so,' Keynes said. 'It would fit in neatly with your theories. But you're quite wrong. It was Lawrence's idea that he should go to town, not mine.'

'At your suggestion.'

'Just his idea.'

'It didn't occur to you to prevent him.'

'Prevent him? Why should I? You placed no restriction on his movements.' Keynes laughed shortly. 'He hasn't run, you know. He'll be back again this evening. His gear and pictures are still at the cottage, and he didn't pack as much as a toothbrush.'

'Then if he's coming back, why did he go?'

Keynes shrugged. 'Your guess is as good as mine. He didn't tell me. But if you say he's dodging you, I'm ready to go along with that. There can be no doubt that you shook him up yesterday, and he wouldn't be looking forward to a repetition.'

Gently stared silently for a moment. 'I don't think Turner is our man,' he said.

'Which makes two of us,' Keynes said. 'Lawrence may be an ass, but he's a harmless ass.'

'He could also have been a tool.'

'Now you've lost me,' Keynes said. 'Though no doubt it redounds to my discredit. But perhaps we should get all that out of the way. At least, it would save you being quite so foxy.'

'You are offering me a confession?' Gently said.

'Not quite a confession,' Keynes grinned. 'But just a look at those facts you were mentioning.' He gestured up the track. 'Shall we walk?'

They continued along the ride, which by now had reached a level. It had also reached a cross-ride, a junction flooded with hot sunlight. Keynes bore right. Here they were passing between sections of Scots and

Corsican. The boles of the Scots were redder, flakier, and there was more of blueness in their shorter needles. Keynes pointed with his stalk to one of the trees, in the crown of which was a raft of dead needles.

'That's a squirrel's drey, in passing. But don't let it interrupt our conversation.'

He strode on easily for another fifty yards.

'You know, I'm quite your best bet,' he said. 'I know that Lawrence has a lot going for him, but mostly it's just the foolish way he's behaved. Now I add up on every count. It's a fact that I would like to marry Maryon. I have been in love with her for a long time—pretty well as soon as she came here, in fact. So there is a Lloyd's A-1 motive, though it's arguable that I didn't have to kill Adrian—still, put it along with the money, and call it demented infatuation, and all that. Lawrence has nothing to match it, has he?'

'He would if he were marrying Miss Britton,' Gently grunted.

'Yes,' Keynes smiled. 'But that is still rather hypothetical. Jennifer is chummy with him, true, but I doubt if her intentions are very serious. So you had better admit it—I'm the hot one. A breath of proof, and I'd be inside.'

Gently said nothing.

'Agreed,' Keynes said. 'And now, take a look at my opportunity. Lawrence has left, Jenny has gone to bed, and I'm left alone with Maryon. Well, Maryon is *the* interested party, so it's a fair bet that she wouldn't stop me; more likely, you can argue, she played the Lady Macbeth, and nerved my sluggish hand to the deed.' He glanced quickly at Gently. 'Do you so argue?'

Gently hunched his shoulders silently.

'Let's say it has occurred to you,' Keynes said. 'It

would have done to me, in your place. However, the premise isn't wholly necessary, since Maryon may well have gone up before me, or I may have hood-winked her with some clever excuse for going out again that night. Of course, she would suspect later, though even now she may not be sure. But she would certainly give me an alibi to keep me out of trouble with people like you.'

Gently hesitated. '*Did* you go out?'

Keynes grinned broadly. 'Would it put me inside?'

Gently stared at him: Keynes grinned back. Then he held up the stalk, a sort of token between them.

'No, I didn't, except to lock up the car. I was about to retire with Maryon, remember. She would scarcely have gone to bed without me, or have accepted my cleverest excuse for going out. But this has to remain as surmise on your part. The facts are that I had lyrical opportunity. It boils down to myself, or Maryon, or both of us, and a betting man could only take me. That's your opinion, isn't it?'

Gently walked a few paces. 'Are you going to tell me how you knew where to find him?'

Keynes smiled at his stalk. 'That's the big problem, of course. How I could manoeuvre him to Mogi's Belt.' He gestured with the stalk. 'I would have to get to him somehow, and in a friendly sort of way—make him forget we'd had a cataclysmic row, and enthuse him with shooting a film of badgers.' He laughed sud-denly. 'But yes—I see now! That's what you were hinting at earlier on. I used Lawrence. He didn't row with Adrian. He was my tool to get Adrian out there.' He looked admiringly at Gently. 'Have I hit on the answer?'

'You seem to think so,' Gently said.

'But it fits so neatly,' Keynes laughed. 'And frank-ly, it could have happened just like that. There was a bit of a relation between Lawrence and Adrian.

Lawrence is at an age to worship success. It flattered Adrian. He had Lawrence stay in town with him. You couldn't have hit on a more likely solution.' He checked himself, his smile thinning. 'But no, you have to be wrong,' he said. 'That row was in the air, it affected Lawrence too. He would scarcely have picked then to tell Adrian such a thing.'

'Unless he was persuaded to,' Gently said.

Keynes shook his head and said nothing. The smile had gone out of his eyes. He strode silently for some moments.

'But . . . when all the kidding is over.'

'Yes?' Gently said.

'When you've finished sniffing round us, you'll do well to take a look at the other end.'

'Precisely which other end?'

Keynes's shoulders twitched. 'I suppose it has to start with Walling. But I wouldn't entirely exclude his daughter, or the pot-fringe that comes with her. The motive may be obscure, perhaps scarcely credible —like gassing Adrian for kicks. But that's not impossible. It would be in line with the level of decadence you find there.' He grinned wryly. 'You could say they felled too many trees when they built London. Now the place is going slowly mad. Quod erat demonstrandum.'

'Is that just a general suggestion,' Gently said, 'or do I get names?'

Keynes shook his head. 'I don't know their names. But your smell is as good as mine.'

Now they had reached the full glare of sunlight where a complete section was naked of trees. Instead it was sown with short meadow grass with soft, downy flower-heads, as purple as heather. Trenching was visible, however, stretching faint furrows across the expanse, and in the shelter of the furrows, almost hidden by herbage, were tiny saplings, only inches tall. Here were wildflowers in plenty. The section was fringed with viper's bugloss, and rashes of its chalky blue flowers and crimson buds showed distantly in the purple glass. Campions, white and red, scabious, knapweed and wild mignonette, milfoil, vetchling and yellow trefoil flowered riotously beside the track. Here too was a diversity of butterflies, Walls, Ringlets, Meadow Browns, Orange Tips, Common Blues, Tortoiseshells, Heaths and Skippers. But most surprising was the colour of the grass and the soft uniformity of its sweep, as though the section had been painted over with a full, unhesitating brush.

Keynes gave Gently one of his little quick glances as they turned right again, between trees and meadow.

'Here's the true sanity,' he said. 'Here Samsara *is* Nirvana.'

'A pity Stoll can no longer appreciate it,' Gently said dryly.

'Yes, a pity,' Keynes said. 'Though Adrian was a child of the dualities. He would have wanted to take a photograph.'

'And that's how you remember him?'

Keynes shook his head. 'I wish he were here, under this sun. Taking photographs, if he wanted to, and laying down the law to everyone. But since he's dead—well, he's dead, as you and I will be at last, and the pity is he's left a problem and bad karma for someone. But crime punishes itself, you know, irrespective of you fellows.'

'Perhaps,' Gently said. 'But we still have a use, if it's only to stop the criminals from punishing themselves. Or would that be contrary to the Tao?'

Keynes grinned, and tossed his stalk at Gently.

'In a way,' he said, 'Adrian died well—doing what he wanted, at the height of his powers. He was prevented from making himself some bad karma, and perhaps from artistic decline. He enjoyed himself, and slept. Life should be so kind to all of us.'

'In a way,' Gently said. 'But we're left with a killer.'

'And the killer is left with himself,' Keynes said.

'You would leave it like that?'

Keynes shook his head. 'Because the killer, too, is Buddha.'

'So we catch him,' Gently said. 'And that's his way back—perhaps knocking a kalpa out of the reckoning. And meanwhile preserving him from fresh bad karma, like being the happy release of further Stolls.'

Keyes chuckled. 'I hear what you say.'

'Then perhaps now you'll give me a name,' Gently said.

'If I could, I would,' Keynes said. 'And your wisdom now is to believe me.' He looked steadily at Gently. 'Or to try to,' he said. 'Keeping your suspicion in a separate compartment.'

Gently stared back. 'We *shall* catch him,' he said.

'To believe which,' Keynes said, 'is *my* wisdom.'

They passed the meadow, which was succeeded by a section of feathery, droop-skirted larches, at the foot of which young beeches spread level leaves to the filtered sun. Still on the right were the cool chambers of the Corsicans, a benevolent recession of pinkish-grey shafts, below which a few deciduous seedlings peered wistfully at the little sky. All was silent, except for the far-off broken clamour of a cuckoo.

Ahead, a figure turned out a cross-ride.

'Look—there's Maryon!' Keynes said.

Maryon Britton waved uncertainly, then made up her mind and hurried towards them. Keynes hastened ahead. They met smilingly, standing for a moment before each other. She was dressed in a simple, sleeveless print frock, which became her better than the suit of yesterday.

'I thought I would find you round here!' She turned to Gently, her smile dying. 'And you.' But the smile half-returned. 'He said you'd be human if he took you into the forest.'

'Oh, he's human anyway,' Keynes grinned. 'It doesn't need a lot of bringing out.'

'Well, it didn't show much yesterday,' Maryon Britton said. 'And certainly not in the way he treated poor Lawrence.'

She fell into step between them, lengthening her stride to keep time with theirs. She walked with an easy, graceful step: the natural gait of a country-woman.

'Tell me the truth,' she said to Gently. 'You haven't secretly arrested Lawrence, have you?'

Gently shrugged. 'An arrest is public,' he said. 'No, we haven't arrested Turner.'

'Well, Jenny thinks you have,' Maryon Britton said. 'He went off this morning without seeing her. So she suspects that you came after him and that I'm trying to keep it from her.'

'Dear Jenny,' Keynes smiled. 'But she won't be a teenager much longer.'

'It can't be over too soon,' Maryon Britton said. 'Being mothers and daughters is a wearing business.'

'But would he normally have seen her?' Gently asked.

'Most mornings,' Maryon Britton said. 'At least he could have rung. He should know by now what a little goose my daughter is.'

Keynes sent Gently a glance over Maryon Britton's head. 'Lawrence was still a bit dopey this morning,' he said. 'Which isn't surprising. Being put through the ropes yesterday must have given him the shock of his young life. But he was recovering. I dare say a whirl in the big city will complete the cure. There's a gallery in the Bush I told him about—I know he was keen to follow it up.'

'What time did he leave?' Gently asked.

'Straight after breakfast—around nine.' Keynes hesitated. 'He had to pick up petrol, so no doubt he would call at the garage.'

'Really, he's as idiotic as Jenny,' Maryon Britton said. 'The kids today have no stability. What that girl needs is a father figure.' She flashed a smile at Keynes. 'But not you, Edwin.'

They turned down the ride from which Maryon Britton had emerged, and which at length led them back to the church. The white shape of the Lotus waited poised and fish-like, its enamel still glowing with Central Office polish. Gently unlocked it.

'Can I offer you a lift?'

Maryon Britton shook her head. 'Not if you've finished with us. I intend to seduce Edwin away from his typewriter. That is, if he had any intention of returning to it.'

Keynes shrugged a negative. 'I'm a weakling,' he said. 'My reviews can wait till rainy weather.'

'So thanks,' Maryon Britton said. 'It's an awfully nice car. But we'll continue our stroll to the river.'

Gently got in and slammed the door. They stood by watching while he started the engine. He turned the Lotus in a tight circle on the plot before the church: his mirror showed them still watching as he drove away.

9

He took the main road into the village, which lay deserted and drowsing in the brilliant sunlight. It had a graceless, lopsided street which cranked at a right angle by a patch of green. Also there was a square, bounded on three sides by old-fashioned shops and an inn; rather happy-go-lucky. People lived there, and the picturesque came in by accident.

Gently pulled in at the garage, where there was just room to park beside delivery lines that swung out on arms. A man appeared, massive and greasy in oil-plated dungarees. He looked at the Lotus, then at Gently.

'Only four star, old partner,' he said.

'That'll do,' Gently said. 'Fill her up.'

'Right you are,' the man said, reaching for a line.

Gently climbed out and lounged by the car. 'Which way is Deerview Cottage?' he asked.

The man glanced up briefly from his gushing nozzle. 'Turn right up here by the green,' he said. He slid Gently another look. 'That's Ted Keynes's place,' he said. 'But I reckon you won't find him in. I saw him come past here a time back.'

'It's his friend I'm looking for,' Gently said.

'Ah,' the man said. 'Young Lawrence. But he's out too. He was in here earlier, driving the car. I gave him a fill-up.'

'Which way was he heading?' Gently asked.

'Why, going town-way,' the man said. 'But where he was heading I never asked him. I just know he had a tank of juice.'

Gently paid and idled away, but neglected to turn right by the green. Instead he continued along the street to where the houses became larger and more affluent-looking. At the church he hesitated briefly, then turned down towards the forest. He glided the Lotus through the Lodge gates and let it roll to a stop by the side-door.

The side-door was open, as it had been yesterday, but this time Gently had to ring. He heard the sound of footfalls on the stairs before Jennifer Britton appeared in the passage. She was dressed in jeans and a sleeveless shirt. There was redness and puffiness about her eyes. She came forward reluctantly, her eyes wary, and stopped a pace inside the door.

'Have you—come for me, too?'

Gently smiled and shook his head. 'Just to tell you not to worry about Lawrence.'

'But you've got him, haven't you?'

'No. It's as you were told. He borrowed Mr Keynes's car and drove to London.'

She caught at a strand of blonde hair. 'But you'd lie to me anyway. That's the way you get people to talk.'

Gently shrugged. 'Then your mother is lying too, and Mr Keynes. We must all be in it.'

She stood regarding him suspiciously for a few moments, but then timidly advanced to the brick step. Her hair looked ragged and unbrushed, and there were stains of tears on her thin cheeks.

'If you haven't got him, then where is he?'

'By his own account he was going to London.'

'But Lawrence doesn't know anybody in London! And why would he go without telling me?'

'Would he have told you?'

'Yes—of course! I might have wanted to go with

him. In fact, I probably would have gone with him.'

'Perhaps that's why he didn't tell you.'

She chewed her lip. 'It's your fault, anyway. You *know* that Lawrence didn't do it. You've just been laying into Lawrence and hoping that someone else will confess.'

'Who else, Miss Britton?'

She eyed him sullenly. 'It wouldn't be Edwin, of course, would it? He's much too clever! If he killed Adrian you may as well give up now. And Mother, it wouldn't be her, because Mother knows how to get round you. Mother is an *actress,* or haven't you noticed? She's never been known to fluff a line.' She leaned against the doorpost, squinting up at him. 'Why haven't you been questioning *me?*' she said. 'Oh, not just taking a silly statement, but really grilling me—like Lawrence?' She thrust her face forward. '*Why* haven't you? That's what I'm finding so very strange.'

Gently sighed. 'Have you the keys to the Imp?'

'No—but I could have borrowed Lawrence's.'

'Or used the Rapier?'

'No—yes, because I cleaned it jolly soon afterwards.'

'Then you would have cleaned the Imp, if you'd used that.'

'Well, that could have been to divert suspicion. To make you think it was really Edwin, who is quite capable of looking after himself.'

'So you want me to suppose that you are the culprit?'

She breathed deeply. 'Yes. And you keep ignoring me.'

Gently shook his head slowly. 'Not ignoring you, Miss Britton. When you seem so certain that your friend is guilty.'

She went suddenly white: as though he had slapped her. 'But that—that's ridiculous!' she stammered.

'Not at all, Miss Britton. Lawrence Turner loves you. You find it quite credible that he would do this thing.'

'But I *know* he didn't!'

Gently hunched. 'On the contrary. I'm beginning to think you may know he *did*. Because before suspicion ever turned towards Turner, you were trying to draw it towards yourself.'

She gave a little gasp, and for a moment gazed round-eyed, her small mouth open, showing teeth. But then, in the distant quietness of the hall, the telephone began to ring.

'Lawrence!'

She sprang back into the house, her fair hair flying. Gently followed. She snatched up the phone, a triumphant smile on her pale face.

'Yes—it's me!'

But the smile vanished, lapsed into a sullen, baffled expression.

'Oh . . . yes. Hold on.' She held out the phone to Gently. 'Yours.'

Gently took it. The caller was Metfield.

'I wondered if I'd catch you, sir,' he said. 'We've just had a couple of visitors who I thought you'd like to see.'

Gently grunted. 'What visitors?'

'Two from London, sir,' Metfield said. 'There's the actress, Miss Walling, and a TV writer, Ivan Webster.'

'What do they want?'

'I don't quite know, sir. Shall I tell them you're on your way?'

Gently nodded to the gloom of the hall. 'Yes. You can certainly tell them that.'

Outside the police station stood Webster's Volvo, bronze and black, with London grime on it. No hint of redness in its dust-film, or revealing stain on its fat

Michelins. Gently brooded round it for a while, studying the small scars, the cluttered interior. He tried a
door; it had been left unlocked—and dumped in the
back was a Leica camera. He slammed the door and
went into the station, where the desk-sergeant nodded
towards Metfield's office.

Webster sat sprawled on a chair by the window,
smoking a cigarette in an amber holder. He was
dressed in tight-waisted bell-bottom trousers and a
sheepskin coat, with no shirt under it. On a chair by
the filing-cabinets sat Nina Walling, in a gown that
fell straight from shoulder to heel. Its deep V-neck
reached almost to her navel and revealed the naked-
ness of small breasts. She too was smoking: she had
a long jet holder. Neither took any notice of Gently's
entrance.

Metfield rose from the desk, where he'd been toying
with paper-work, to leave the seat of honour to Gently. Gently took it. Webster reached languidly to the
window and flicked ash into the M/T yard. He turned
with slow, lazy arrogance.

'How's life in the country, fuzz?' he drawled. 'Like
it's so peaceful here, in the depths. Even the fuzz-
scene is relaxed.'

'You have some business?' Gently said.

'Yah, yah,' Webster drawled. 'Though mostly it's
just a social call. But you can say we have business
too.'

'Well?'

Webster gestured to Nina Walling.

'We want to know where my father stands,' she said
chillily. 'All this time he is being hounded by you
people, if not for one thing then for another. So we
want this business cleared up, at least, before he becomes a nervous wreck. And every time we inquire
of Inspector Lyons he refers us to you.'

Webster nodded his bush of hair. 'That's the curve, fuzz. Why we hit the rural scene.'

'By now,' Nina Walling said, 'you've surely made some progress. So we can expect a positive statement.'

Her green eyes probed at Gently: small eyes in a small face. But set regally, on a long neck: a little snake-like. And cold.

'Did your father send you?' Gently asked.

'My father is occupied with assisting the police. They have taken over his business premises and they might just as well have taken over the flat. My father is ruined. I am trying to prevent him from becoming a mental wreck as well.'

'But did he send you?'

'No, he didn't.'

'Like he's too hung up, fuzz,' Webster said. 'You should be up there giving it the action. He'd tell you anything you wanted to hear.'

'He is in a highly disturbed state,' Nina Walling said. 'And it's time he was shown some mercy.'

She inhaled smoke and nostrilled it, letting her eyes slide past Gently's. Webster's eyes were narrowed, peering from behind eaves of hair.

'Your father's position is still being investigated,' Gently said. 'We have reasons for continuing our interest.'

'But not for hounding him,' Nina Walling said. 'Which is what you are doing to him now.'

Gently shrugged. 'We have to ask him to help us. His account of his movements has not been verified. He was plainly under some threat from Mr Stoll. We have learned nothing yet that excludes your father.'

Webster guffawed. 'That's levelling, fuzz!'

'Only it's nonsense!' Nina Walling snapped sharply. 'You know, we all know where Daddy went—he had been visiting that creature in Brighton for years.

Daddy kept him, did you know that? Just like another
man might keep a woman. And he pretended to have a
sister there, to deceive Nigel—just as another man
might deceive his wife! Isn't that true, Ivan?'

'The truest,' Webster said. 'Oscar's been cheating
on Nigel for ever. And like everyone knows but
Nigel. Isn't that a sweet situation for a deadpan
script?'

Gently shook his head. 'It doesn't help,' he said.
'It would have been better if Vivian Chance had
been a stranger. If he is being kept, then his witness
is suspect. And we have found nothing to support it.'

'Oh, how ridiculous!' Nina Walling exclaimed.

'We could say he was at home, fuzz,' Webster
drawled. 'Just, like, to get you off the hook with Oscar,
who sure as satan didn't kill Adrian. I was at the
flat till after midnight.'

Gently flicked a look at him. 'How long after?'

'Yah—about,' Webster drawled. 'Could have been
half-past, or getting for one.' He let his eyes hood.
'I'll add it up, fuzz. I got to the Capri at eleven.
That was before the curtain came down, like maybe
five or ten minutes to go. Then Nina cleans up and
dresses, and there's drinks and chatter, you know,
and there's twenty minutes to Campden Hill, and
ten minutes' chat when we get there.' He opened his
eyes wide again. 'Call it one a.m.—like I could make
it stand up in court, fuzz. Then just as I'm leaving,
in comes Oscar, who has changed his mind about staying at Brighton—and man, he's tired with all that
driving, he goes straight in to hit the sack.' He looked
mockingly at Gently. 'Any help to you, fuzz?'

Gently stared. 'What happened next?'

Webster's grey eyes gleamed. 'You're being unkind,
fuzz. Like I'm only trying to straighten you out.'

'So tell me what happened.'

'I love him,' Webster said. 'I went home to my

sack too. Across the river in old Battersea, a seagull's poop from Father Thames. Any comeback?'

Gently said nothing.

'I love all fuzz,' Webster said. 'They bring out the mother in me. Getting bust by fuzz is like sexual.'

Nina Waling snatched her head impatiently. 'But all this is so much nonsense! Daddy was in Brighton, that's flat, and obviously you believe it too. Because if you don't, why are you here, and leaving Daddy to a subordinate? It's because you expect an arrest at this end, and from all I know, you're absolutely right.'

'Then you no longer believe that Mr Stoll committed suicide?'

'That was my theory, fuzz,' Webster said. 'It could be either way, but if it's a killing, then you have to agree with Nina. Somebody out here stood to lose a lot, and that somebody knew where to find Adrian. Like it sticks out past Christmas. You aren't even trying to hang it on Oscar.'

'In that case, Mr Walling has nothing to worry about.'

'Yeah,' Webster said. 'But he has. Oscar is too hung up to be thinking sense. He has to know for sure that you've crossed him off.'

Gently slowly shook his head. 'I can't give Mr Walling clearance. Not even if he did happen to be in Brighton.'

'Even if we could prove it to you?' Nina Walling snapped.

'That fact alone doesn't clear him.'

They gazed at Gently: Nina Walling furiously, Webster with alert probing eyes.

'Yeah?' he said. 'How's that?'

Gently shrugged, and swivelled his chair to face away from them.

'Your father is a man of wide connections, Miss Walling. In the spectrum of finance they come in all colours. At certain levels a man's life is a commodity, and it was one that your father could easily afford.'

'But that—that's just *crazy*!' Nina Walling burst out.

'Not at all, Miss Walling. We think it very likely.'

'But you can't—it's ludicrous!'

'The pattern is familiar. And your father was a desperate man.'

'Oh boy!' Webster said. 'Oh boy!'

'Listen,' Nina Walling said. 'It's just utterly fantastic! Daddy doesn't mix with that sort of people. All right, he knows plenty who have been on the fiddle, but not thugs and murderers. Daddy isn't like that. He's a *refined* person. He has a horror of violence and violent people. You just don't know him, that's all, and it's so ridiculous that I could weep.'

'You are convinced that your father has no criminal connections?'

'Oh lord—yes, yes!'

Gently swung back to her. 'So that would leave us with amateur confederates. Which the style of the crime seems to suggest.'

Her green eyes popped at him: her mouth set tight. Two points of pallor appeared over her cheekbones.

Webster gave a sardonic chuckle. 'Nicely taken, fuzz!' he said softly.

'You follow my point?' Gently said.

'Yah, yah, she follows it,' Webster said. 'Like Oscar had friends who might have helped out. No need to take a sledgehammer, fuzz.'

Gently's eyes stayed fixed on Nina Walling's. 'Friends or acquaintances,' he said. 'Among them some who were no friends of Mr Stoll's, perhaps some who believed he had done them an injury. And among those people one more callous, more vindictive than the rest: one with a deep and permanent resentment, perhaps freshly inflamed by recent developments. Does that suggest anyone to you, Miss Walling? Among your father's acquaintances—and yours?'

Webster laughed harshly. 'Say the odd two dozen, or like anyone who Adrian had been working with lately.'

Nina Walling was staring with eyes in which the pupils had gone small.

'One special person,' Gently persisted. 'Because probably it was only the one person—who may have suggested the measure to your father: may have counted on your father taking the blame?'

'Oh, he's so lovely,' Webster said. 'What a shame it's only a dream, fuzz.'

'Wouldn't you know him?' Gently said. 'Would it be possible for you *not* to know him?'

Nina Walling opened her mouth and closed it again. Her long fingers twitched at her loose gown. Her eyes winced and tried to drag clear, but Gently held them in a steady stare.

'I . . . it's so *senseless*!' She faltered, at last.

'Tell me the name of that person, Miss Walling.'

'No . . . there is no person! Daddy wouldn't . . . it's unthinkable.'

'But someone you suspect—though your father is innocent?'

'No!' She began mechanically shaking her head.

'Someone you know, with a different motive?'

'No—nobody! It's all nonsense.'

'Oh these fuzz, these fuzz,' Webster jeered. 'Like how they try to pitch a curve. Jacking the words into your mouth for you. Pulling a deal out of nowhere. Why not ask me the questions, fuzz?'

Gently swivelled quickly. 'Right. I'm asking.'

'And like I'm going to give you a tip, fuzz. Just keep up the pressure on Lawrence Turner.'

'Turner.' Gently sat quite still. 'What do you know about Turner?'

'Am I hitting the mark?' Webster crowed. 'Maybe your fuzz-eye is on him already.' He leered through his tent of hair. 'I know Lawrence Turner,' he said. 'Met him when I've been down here at the Lodge, then a time or two up in town. He was big with Adrian, know that, fuzz? And Adrian was very big with him. But Adrian wasn't as big as Jennifer Britton, who was, like, going to be turned out in the rain. And Turner's a queer kid, you know that? He flips his lid at low temperature. He flipped in a pub bar one night and it took three of us to hold him. So that's my tip, fuzz. Lean on Turner. He's the cat who's most likely. Maybe there's others who have a finger in it, but Lawrence Turner is your gasman.' He sprawled back against the window, eyes mocking, though still alert.

'Thank you,' Gently said dryly.

'Yah, I love all fuzz,' Webster said. 'So like now you can stop bullying Nina, and even give her what she came for.'

'The answer is still the same,' Gently said.

'Which is a right buzz-fuzz answer,' Webster said. 'And you can stuff it, because you've let out one thing. You're seeing the action from out here.'

'From everywhere,' Gently said. 'I hope.'

'Yah, but Turner in close shot,' Webster said. 'You didn't need that tip from me, because Turner is where you've got your dough.' He came up off the chair. 'You through with him, Nina?'

'Oh lord, yes,' Nina Walling said. 'I've had all the policemen I can take for one morning. This one isn't so subtle after all.' She rose too.

'Bye, bye,' Webster said. 'Always a pleasure to chat up the fuzz. If you step across to the Sun I'll buy you a lunch—like swede salad with roast pig.'

He opened the door. Gently said nothing. Webster

held it open for Nina Walling. Nina Walling swept through, her chin in the air, and Webster leered before following her out. The door closed; Gently reached for his pipe. He began to fill it with deliberate fingers.

A couple of minutes passed and the pipe was going before Metfield ventured on a comment. Then he rose, lightly flexed his muscles, and came to perch on a corner of the desk. He looked wistfully at Gently.

'Are you thinking what I'm thinking?'

'What are you thinking?' Gently said.

'I'm thinking I'd like to work that chummie over. Also that he knows a lot more than he's told us.'

Gently nodded over his pipe. 'Those are roughly my sentiments. He knows what makes this scene tick.'

'And about Turner,' Metfield said. 'Especially about Turner. I reckon he could give us Turner, if he had a mind to.' He paused, snapping his fingers. 'Did Webster seem a bit familiar to you, sir?'

Gently glanced at him curiously. 'A bit. I've been puzzling to think where I might have seen him.'

Metfield's thick features folded in a grin. 'You saw him here, sir. In Latchford. But that would be thirteen years ago, so it's small wonder you couldn't place him.'

Gently gripped his pipe tightly. 'He was one of that crowd?'

'Yes, sir. One of the Jeebies. Used to ride around with Dicky Deeming, who killed himself in Five Mile Drove. But Webster was only a stringer, sir, so perhaps you wouldn't have seen much of him.'

Gently drew some fierce puffs. 'Tell me what you know about Webster.'

'Yes, sir,' Metfield said. 'He's a Londoner, properly, his family moved up here with the first overspill.

Webster was a Teddie when he came here, then he
kind of graduated to the Jeebies—Speed Twin, black
leathers, all that sort of caper.'

'Any record?' Gently said.

'Just speeding a few times,' Metfield said regret-
fully. 'He wasn't in that punch-up in the Market
Place, when they tried to snatch Bixley off you.
Then after you'd cracked that bunch it wasn't too
clever to go around as a Jeebie anymore, so Webster
traded his bike for a scooter. A while after that he
left town.'

'But his people still live here?' Gently said.

'Well, in the district,' Metfield said. 'His father,
Jack Webster, got promotion, and that meant him
shifting out to Sanford. He's a Forestry man.'

'A *what*?'

'Forestry,' Metfield said. 'Assistant District Con-
servator. That's well up the ladder. So now he's living
at the Forestry Centre, at Sanford.'

Gently gazed at the local man for an instant: then
he grabbed the case file from Metfield's tray. He
slipped out the Trail pamphlet and spread it open
to reveal the last page of the text.

'Look!'

He jabbed a commanding commanding forefinger.
Metfield leaned across and goggled. Where the text
ended, at the foot of the page, ran a minute super-
scription:

'L62/2271/JW'

Metfield swallowed his tongue twice. 'This . . . are
you saying Jack Webster wrote it?'

'Wrote it—discussed it—perhaps got some help with
it—from a son who just happens to be a writer!'

Metfield's tongue went through it again. 'I'll get
him on the phone, sir. I know Jack Webster to talk
to.'

Gently shook his head impatiently. 'Never mind Jack Webster. Just get to work on the office door.'

'The—office door?'

'The office door! Which chummie had his hands on ten minutes ago.' Gently leaned back, a smile shaping in his eyes. 'Somehow, I've the feeling we're about to win one.'

Metfield bustled out. He returned quickly with a D.C. carrying a camera and gear. Together they puffed powder over the door in the neighbourhood of the knobs. No shortage of latents! The D.C. took the photographs and stripped instant-prints from the camera; then each of them sat down with a pair of photographs and a copy of the pamphlet dab from a file. The D.C. was the lucky one.

'This looks like a match, sir.'

The two photographs were pushed across to Gently. Metfield and his aide clustered, one at each shoulder, as Gently made the comparison with a magnifier. At the seventh point of similarity he laid down the glass.

'This should be enough to go on with. Present my compliments to Mr Ivan Webster, lurching at the Sun, and ask him to step round for a further conversation.'

'Just a further conversation, sir?' the D.C. queried.

'In friendlywise,' Gently said. 'Let him feel wanted.'

The D.C. left. Metfield sat down heavily, and was silent for a while.

10

Webster returned alone.

He came into the office carrying some cold chicken between two plates; set it down on the typist's table, drew up a chair, and began eating, without a word. Gently said nothing; Metfield stared affrontedly. Webster gnawed at a drumstick held between his fingers; there was something savage about him. He crouched over the plate, his hair brushing it, his eyes intent. He dealt with the drumstick, then burped.

'No objection, fuzz?' he inquired cheerfully. 'Only, like, we have to be back in town, on account of Nina has a show to do.'

'No objection,' Gently said. 'And you're free to leave when you wish.'

'Yah?' Webster said. 'So what's the curve? Why have you grabbed me away from lunch?'

Gently gestured casually. 'It seems I should know you.'

Webster sank his teeth into a wing. His grey eyes stared hard at Gently. Gently sat back relaxedly in the swivelling desk chair.

'Yah,' Webster said. He chewed for a while. 'Like you're a slow starter,' he said. 'I remembered you, fuzz, but who wouldn't? All that free promotion you get, too.'

Gently ducked his head. 'It makes a difference,' he said. 'And then again, you were one of a crowd. Yet there was something in your style that clicked. The way you talk. Perhaps the way you think.'

Webster chewed. 'Is that needle, fuzz?'

Gently made a face. 'Call it curiosity. Deeming made a deep impression on the kids who ran with him. I'm curious to know how it wears.'

Webster tore off a strip with his teeth. 'Like you never caught up with that cat,' he said, chewing. 'So he went for the touch, he kept going. But that just left you holding fresh air.'

'He was a killer,' Gently said.

'Yah?' Webster said. 'That was the jazz the fuzz put around. But like who believed it? You were out to bust Dicky, so when you lost him, what would you say?' He went on chewing. 'Dicky was the greatest,' he said. 'Far out. You couldn't forgive him.'

Gently hunched. 'He had original ideas.'

'Like better than original,' Webster said. 'Dicky was touching all along, fuzz. You read that posthumous book of his?'

'I read it,' Gently said.

'You read it,' Webster said. 'And like you're as square now as you were then. Still living along with the drag society, a hung-up square, beating heads.' He threw the wing bones on the plate, picked up another drumstick and bit into it.

'But for you, those ideas are valid,' Gently said.

Webster chewed. 'They're valid, period. Dicky's jazz about aesthetics, about living on the borders. That's crazy valid. Because the action's there, fuzz, along the borders. That's where you get the on-off kick. Like in between is the big drag, the kicks are spaced along the seams.'

'Where contrasts meet.'

Webster nodded. 'Crazy.'

'Like light and dark, sound and silence.'

'Yah, now you're getting it,' Webster said.

'Lawful and unlawful.'

Webster chewed.

'But then it went deeper,' Gently said. 'Like Deeming's distrust of the intellect. His tendency to enthrone the intuition, to give it unrestricted control. That's a form of Zen with the stopper off. It becomes dangerous when taught to the young and undisciplined. And if you add to it an aesthetic philosophy based on ecstasy, then a creed of violence is the probable result.'

Webster took a fresh bite, chewed, swallowed. 'Only Dicky didn't go for violence,' he said. 'He kept it cool, you remember? Cool, cool. That was the message.'

Gently nodded. 'Yes, I remember. Deeming thought his discipline was equal to the strain. But unhappily it wasn't, and under pressure he resorted to violence as soon as the next man—sooner perhaps, because he had trained himself to act without intellection. That was Deeming's creed in action: killing Lister didn't break the rules. Which is why I'm curious to know how the creed is wearing, thirteen years after Deeming's death.'

'Yah,' Webster said, 'yah.' He threw down the drumstick and licked his fingers. He looked round the table, took a sheet of typing paper, polished his fingers, then aimed the ball at the waste-can. 'You know something, fuzz?'

'Tell me,' Gently said.

'You're not so smart as Dicky,' Webster said. 'Dicky could have wound me round his little finger, which is something you're never going to do. Not that Dicky ever did. Dicky gave it to us straight. I got the message from the guru, fuzz. And you, you're like seeing it all from the outside, dressing it up in the square jazz. So how would you know? What's with us discussing it? Like I'll be on my way back to town.'

'You can go,' Gently said.

'Oh sure, sure.' Webster pushed back his hair and stared at Gently. His narrow features had a gaunt look, ended in a lank jaw, a bony chin. He licked his lips and smacked them, but made no move to rise.

'So you worked with Stoll for four years,' Gently said slowly.

'Yah, Stoll,' Webster said. 'Four years.'

'You knew him socially.'

Webster picked at his teeth. 'Yah. If you can call it that.'

'You spent evenings at his flat?'

'Like working evenings. Knocking the rough out of the script. Sometimes he had cast there, and odd cats. It could get to be like a party.'

'Then you'd go on location with him?'

'Right. Only nobody would call that a party.'

'And sometimes he invited you to the Lodge.'

'Sometimes,' Webster said. 'Just sometimes.'

'So you probably knew him better than most.'

'Why not?' Webster drew a can of beer from the pocket of his sheepskin; he tore off the flap and tossed it at the waste-can, then sucked a mouthful of beer. Gently waited.

'Why not,' Webster repeated. 'Yah, I'll buy it. I knew Adrian better than most. Like I said, we had a kind of relation, or as near as he'd let you get to one.'

'Was he queer?'

Webster's eyes flickered. 'That's a lovely curve to throw,' he said softly. 'Man, wouldn't that tie in with Oscar, and, like, his regular boy friend, Nigel? Because queers do tend to flip and freak—yah, that Nigel is a quiet cat. I could see *him* tailing off Adrian with some hose and a bottle of gas. It's a nice pitch.' He laughed.

'*Was* Stoll queer?' Gently said.

Webster sucked beer. 'That's the hang-up,' he said. 'I never did see any signs of it.' He laughed again. 'Even straight, you wouldn't call Adrian a compulsive sexer. And he had it around, lots of dollies who would have laid him from now till breakfast. Like Adrian was old-fashioned, a one-at-a-timer—monogamy, didn't they use to call it? It went out a way back. Like he was the last of the big oncers.'

'You're saying that Stoll was not promiscuous.'

'Yah, if you want it in yesterday's jazz.'

'He attached himself exclusively to one woman.'

'Man, you love a square mouthful.'

'And currently that woman was Miss Walling.'

Webster stared at Gently across the beer-can. 'Yah, all right. He was hung on Nina. Nobody's going to quarrel with that.'

'For example, his old-fashioned attitude didn't bother you?'

Webster sucked more beer. 'Yah. I'll buy it.'

'It didn't bother you that Stoll was rich, influential in show business, and likely to offer Miss Walling marriage?'

Webster sucked beer quickly. 'Like why should it?' he said. 'Nina wasn't going to jump into a deal like that. Marriage is kaput, is for the birds, we don't make that scene any longer. So she's relating with him, that's real, and he's helping her to orbit. But she's crazy sold on her thing, she wouldn't have cut out with an oldie like Adrian.'

'You were convinced of that?'

'Yah. Convinced.'

'And your relations with Stoll were unaffected.'

'Dead unaffected.'

'I was thinking—professionally. The play for television you were engaged on?'

Webster clutched tight on the beer-can. 'So we had script troubles. Show me the production that never

did. You going to cut confetti from that, you'll have
to bust the entire industry.'

'But amounting to over fifty per cent of the script?'

'Yah—fifty per cent! It does happen.'

'With a director and writer who've worked together for four years?'

'Yah—yah—it happens. Even then!'

'But surely, not without a reason?'

Webster glared at him, his mouth twisting. His
fingers clenched and unclenched on the beer-can,
making the thin metal creak.

'Are you saying Adrian was cutting me down, fuzz?'

'I was waiting to hear your comment.'

'Like that's what you're saying! On account of
maybe I've ridden along with him till now.'

Gently shrugged. 'And you haven't?'

'No! Not so as he could cut me down. I've sold
stuff here, there and all over, as well as going along
with Adrian.'

'Then the failure of his patronage was of no con-
sequence.'

'Right! I can earn my bread any day.'

'His influence could not have affected that.'

'His influence—!' Webster slammed the beer-can
at the floor. He crouched towards Gently, eyes fero-
cious. 'You bastard,' he said. 'You're trying to fix me.
Like you don't give a fart who did it for real, as
long as you finish up with me.'

'Calm down,' Gently said. 'Nobody has accused
you.'

'Yah?' Webster said. 'Then why the needle? You
love me so much because of Dicky, you'll fix me up
if it takes a year.'

Gently shook his head. 'There'll be no fixing.'

'Because you hate me,' Webster said. 'Like just one
look you took at me. And Dicky and all—this is the
pay-off.'

'I'm sorry you think so,' Gently said. 'I asked you back merely for information.'

'Yah, and I'll be buying that,' Webster said. 'The lovely fuzz with their innocent natures.'

Gently shrugged. 'You don't have to stay. You're free to walk out through that door.'

Webster laughed fiercely in his face. But still he made no move to rise.

Instead, he reached for the dribbling beer-can, and took a long, final swig at it. Then, briefly, he held out the beer-can in front of him, as though to demonstrate his hand wasn't trembling. He tossed it to Metfield—whose hand was trembling—and took out a cigarette-case. He fitted a cigarette in the amber holder and struck a light on the office table. He flicked the spent match towards Gently.

'The fuzz was being clever,' he said. 'Clever fuzz. The fuzz was, like, making Ivan lose his cool.' He sent a stream of smoke after the match. 'And what did it buy the fuzz?' he said. 'Nothing it bought them, just nothing. Because like there was nothing to buy. You grab me, fuzz?'

Gently was silent.

'Nothing to buy,' Webster said. 'Ivan was far away in Battersea when someone was turning on the gas. Which is fact, fuzzy hard fact, and like all your needling won't change it. So you can hate my guts sideways.' He hissed more smoke towards Gently.

'Tell me about Friday,' Gently said.

Webster stared bleakly. 'What about Friday?'

'Just give me a rundown. All that happened on that day and evening.'

Webster breathed smoke through his nose. 'You're getting comic, fuzz,' he said. 'There wasn't anything happened Friday, it was just holding Thursday away from Saturday.'

'You worked that day?'

'Oh great, I worked.'

'With Mr Stoll?'

'Like who else? I called in at TV Centre with some rewrite Adrian'd asked for. So then Adrian mulls it over and we make adjustments here and there, and then we try it out on set, and fiddle around a bit more. Then I retire to put it together while Adrian gets on with the rehearsal.'

'That was in the morning?'

'Yah, the morning. After lunch I've nothing to do. Adrian is hung up with cameras and lighting, which maybe is going on all afternoon. So I fetched the car and blew, like just to get a change of scene, and came back around four, when Adrian was into the script again.'

'Where did you go?'

Webster mouthed a smoke ring. 'Like I knocked off a couple of banks.' He drew fresh smoke. 'To Nina's pad. You giving a guess what happened there?'

'I'm willing to try,' Gently said. 'On Friday Miss Walling heard of her father's difficulties. It was a critical and interesting situation. She would certainly wish to discuss it.'

'Critical and interesting,' Webster said. 'Yah, that's your loveliest jazz yet. And you're so right, she wanted to discuss it, weigh up where it left her with Adrian. That was the interesting bit, you know? The critical bit belonged to Oscar. Oscar I didn't see, by the way. Like he was out trying to raise some dough.'

'So the matter was discussed between you?'

'Why not?'

'Wouldn't that tend to leave you in a dilemma?'

'Yah?' Webster said. 'What dilemma? I wasn't owing Adrian fifty grand.'

'This was the dilemma,' Gently said. 'You had either to interfere, or lose Nina. Because clearly the solution to her father's problems was lying in Miss Walling's hands. She could consent to marry Mr Stoll if in return he agreed to reprieve her father, and in those circumstances Mr Stoll would certainly have insisted that she ended her liaison with you. Also, in that event, your professional prospects would probably be prejudiced. So this was the dilemma which faced you on the Friday afternoon.'

Webster was silent for a spell, the cigarette trailing smoke by his face. His hard eyes were staring at the desk, never shifting from the one point. He sat still and a little crouched, with a gleam of sweat on his naked chest. At last he made a flicking motion with the cigarette.'

'Yah, all right,' he said. 'I'll buy it. Like I never tagged the fuzz as stupid, and you've given me reasons that stand up. Yah, sure, that was the size of it, Nina was set for a play at Adrian. And I would have been out, and Adrian might have busted me, because, like, it was Nina who was holding me in. I wasn't Adrian's lover-boy, you know? He was taking it out of me through the script. And, like, once I was out of the package deal, he could have bust me with a lot of people. So I'm buying it, fuzz, going along with you. Only where can you take it from there?'

'You returned to the studios at four p.m.?'

Webster nodded. 'About then.'

'Mr Stoll had work waiting for you?'

'Yah—sort of, like rehearsing a couple of scenes. I'm listening, hearing the words, figuring cuts and rewrite. Then afterwards there's a conference, and that's it for the day.'

'But you did have conversation with Mr Stoll?'

Webster flicked the cigarette. 'That follows.'

'You would, perhaps, accompany him to the canteen, and sit for a while over refreshment.'

'Yah, it's been known,' Webster said.

'Talking of other things beside the script. Just casual, ordinary matters. Like where Mr Stoll could photograph badgers.'

The cigarette rose, and stayed still. 'Very interesting, fuzz,' Webster said. 'Wouldn't that be just the thing to chat Adrian with, and him so crazy about filming wildlife.'

'I think it would,' Gently said. 'I think it would have interested Mr Stoll deeply. I think he would have been eager to know in exact detail where he should go to film these animals. And that would call for information from a local person, and one with access to special sources. Such as an officer in the Forestry. Or the relative of such a man.'

Webster took some quick, deliberate puffs.

'Hand me your ballpen,' Gently said.

'Yah?' Webster said. 'Like why should I?'

'Because I'm asking you for it,' Gently said.

Webster hesitated, then plucked a pen from his pocket and leaned forward to shale it across the desk. He watched malevolently as Gently popped it and stroked red lines across a pad.

'Like it matches something, fuzz?'

'Yes,' Gently said. 'It matches something.'

Webster leered. 'So now isn't it too bad they sell those things a dime a dozen?'

Gently opened the file and took out the Trail pamphlet. He laid it on the desk with the map uppermost. He drew a stroke with the ballpen beside the marking on the map. It matched the marking in colour and width of line. Gently looked at Webster.

'Do you recognize this pamphlet?'

Webster eased back. 'Like you think I ought to?'

'I'm asking you a simple question,' Gently said. 'I would like you to answer it—yes or no.'

Webster stared at Gently, at the pamphlet. Smoke

rose from the cigarette without a waver. Nothing moved in the gaunt face except the calculating grey eyes.

'Yah,' Webster said. 'Nice question, fuzz. Because that pen proves, like, nothing. And that's what I'm supposed to be thinking, isn't it, that not a thing can the fuzz prove.' He gave a nervous laugh. 'Yet somehow I'm feeling that the fuzz have got a trap here. Like I just take another step forward and I shall be dropped on from a great height. So this one I don't buy, fuzz. Yah, I recognize that pamphlet. Why wouldn't I? It was me who wrote it, after my old man roughed it out.' Suddenly, violently, he knocked out the cigarette-butt, and ground it savagely beneath his foot.

'You recognize this particular copy?' Gently said.

'Yah, yah, I recognize it,' Webster said. 'Like I've got a bunch of them at the flat which my old man sent me when they came from the printers. So I gave one to Adrian, why not? This was the scene he lived next door to. And wouldn't he just spot the bit about badgers, and like ask for all the jazz I could give him?'

'Is that what you're saying—that he asked for information?'

Webster nodded fast. 'That's what I'm saying. He took one look at the badger bit and then he was all over me with questions.'

Gently stared. 'When?' he said.

'Yah, that's the next question,' Webster said. He raked at the sweat beading on his chest. 'Like the Monday,' he said. 'Maybe Tuesday.'

'Friday,' Gently said.

'I'm settling for Tuesday.'

'Friday.'

Webster's eyes were hating him. 'So even if it's, like,

Friday, which I don't admit, what's the beef, when it was all so innocent?'

'Friday,' Gently said. 'And it wasn't innocent. You picked up that pamphlet after leaving Nina Walling. You drove to your flat and collected it so you could palm it off on Stoll that day.'

Webster's eyes were murder. 'You have to prove that, fuzz.'

Gently nodded. 'Yes, I think we shall prove it. We'll find witnesses who saw your car at the flat at that time, who saw and perhaps heard you discussing the pamphlet with Stoll.'

'And like that proves it was something not innocent?'

'When set in this context,' Gently said. 'At that time you wouldn't have been going out of your way to perform an act of friendship for Mr Stoll.'

Webster scrubbed violently at his chest. 'You got it all tied up, fuzz, haven't you,' he said. 'It was me who sent Adrian out after badgers, so it was me who followed up with a bottle of gas.'

'You tell me,' Gently said.

'Yah, yah, I'll tell you,' Webster said. 'And I'll tell you you'll have to do a rewrite job, because this is one script that will never get shot.'

"I'm listening,' Gently said.

'Yah, you better,' Webster said. 'Because, like, one, I didn't pick up that pamphlet, I already had it in my briefcase. And, like, two, I was never out of London any time, Saturday or Sunday. So it all falls down, fuzz. You've just got nowhere. I didn't plan it and I didn't do it. So you better kick it around some more, fuzz, and figure how you'll get over that.'

Gently shrugged. 'Your alibi doesn't cover you.'

'You think?' There was triumph in Webster's leer.

'It leaves a gap between midnight and six a.m. You had plenty of time to kill Stoll.'

'And that's just where you've boobed, fuzz.' Webster leaned back, caressing his chest with languid fingers. His lips were grinning. 'You hung too much on it. And like now it's going to blow up in your face.'

'You would like to expand on your previous statement?'

'Yah,' Webster said. 'I would like to expand on it. I wish to tell the fuzz how I was woken by a phone call at like two-thirty on Sunday morning.'

'Go on,' Gently said.

'My pleasure,' Webster said. 'It was a personal call from my agent in Los Angeles—like where it was sometime in the afternoon—with some hopeful news of U.S. sales. Now can you beat that?'

'Name,' Gently said.

'Samuel Rosenberg,' Webster said. 'One-one-oh-five Tijuana Boulevard. You'll have to get the phone number from a directory.'

Gently noted down the name. 'We shall certainly check that.'

'But backwards and forwards,' Webster said. 'Because like it's fireproof, fuzz, and that's what you'll find. It takes all the guessing out of the game.' He leaned his head on one side. 'Square one,' he said. 'It didn't come off because it couldn't. Which leaves us with what I was telling you, fuzz. Keep your beady eye on Lawrence Turner.'

'Yes,' Gently said. 'I heard you before.'

'Now hear me again,' Webster said. 'That cat runs a whole lot deeper than you think, and he didn't get his jazz from Dicky Deeming. He's a cat who flips, a freaky cat, a cat who can jump either side of the wall. But he's not so bright, so like you can trip him, a fuzz like you with all the curves.'

'Any other suggestions?' Gently said.

Webster stropped his nails on his chest. Then he

shook his head. 'You'll get there,' he said. 'You may be square, but you'll surely make it.'

The door was tapped apologetically: a constable entered, rather flustered.

'Yes?' Gently said.

'Sorry to interrupt, sir. But there's a lady in reception asking for this gentleman.'

'Nina,' Webster said. 'Like she's due back in town.' His eyes connected with Gently's mockingly. 'Is that door still open, fuzz,' he said. 'Or like shall I send out for a habeas corpus?'

'That door is still open,' Gently said.

'Yah,' Webster said. 'I must have made a point.' He rose, and stood for a moment flapping his torso with the wings of the sheepskin. 'You know, Dicky liked you, fuzz,' he said. 'Which was kind of wild, the way you were pushing him. Me, I don't have Dicky's nice nature, I like to push back when I get pushed. But just maybe I could relate with you too, give or take an incarnation. Isn't that fun?'

Gently said nothing.

'Yah, yah,' Webster said. 'Just maybe.'

11

The door closed: Metfield jumped up immediately.

'Sir! Do you think we're doing the right thing?'

Gently folded his hands behind his head, leaned back, and grinned at the local man.

'Yes.'

'But that chummie's our man, sir! I could feel it in my guts when you were turning him over. He was out here, he did the job. That alibi of his just must be a fake.'

Gently sighed. 'Not a fake,' he said. 'I'm afraid our friend is too intelligent for that. We're going to find that his phone call is depressingly genuine, at some expense to the British tax-payer.'

'But it could have been set up with the agent, sir, and somebody else have taken the call.'

'That's what we'll be spending the money checking,' Gently said. 'But my guess is that Rosenberg is as pure as the lilies.' He shook his head. 'No. Webster was too confident. He had Rosenberg as his ace in the hole. He knew we must have something when we called him back here, so he kept his shirt-tail flying till he found out what. And now he knows, and now we know: Webster has a copper-bottomed alibi. Also, I looked round his car, which hasn't been washed in the last month.'

Metfield took some paces up and down. 'Look, sir,

I *know* he's our chummie!' he said. 'I don't know how he managed to pull it, but that was the killer who just walked out of here. You could smell him. It was like a bad odour. I had to stop myself knocking him off that chair. You could see him doing it again, any time, and figuring he was that much smarter than the rest of us.'

Gently nodded. 'The Devil's disciple.'

'The Devil himself!' Metfield exclaimed.

'No,' Gently said. 'The Devil I met. He had an appointment with the Gallows Tree, thirteen years back. But he had the same black charisma about him, except that in his case it was original. Webster's is borrowed. Perhaps that's the reason why he is less likeable than Deeming.'

'But he's our chummie,' Metfield said. 'You know he is.'

Gently twitched a shoulder. 'One chummie,' he said. 'There has to be two. The inspiration was Webster's, but apparently his wasn't the hand on the gas bottle.'

Metfield hung on, his eyes rounding. 'You don't think that Miss Walling—?'

Gently shook his head. 'Miss Walling is a chilly and perhaps a callous customer, but I don't quite see her as a killer. In any case, she had less opportunity. She would have had to evade Walling's manservant. Also she would be fatigued after two Saturday performances: on the whole, not an effective agent.'

'Could the manservant be in it, sir?'

'Possibly,' Gently said. 'He has a homosexual relationship with Walling. But I doubt if it would move him to murder for Walling's sake, or whether Webster would trust him if it did. Besides which . . .'

'Yes, sir?' Metfield said.

Gently oscillated the swivel-chair. 'There's the curious matter of the pamphlet in the briefcase—which
seems to point in another direction altogether.'

Metfield did a tongue swallow. 'The pamphlet,
sir . . . ?'

'Yes,' Gently nodded. 'Webster didn't have to fetch
it. He had it with him already. Before his interview
with Miss Walling. Before, you would have thought,
he could know he would need it.'

Metfield opened and closed his mouth. 'Perhaps
that was coincidence. He might have carried one
about just to show people.'

'It seems scarcely likely,' Gently said. 'When he
wasn't responsible even for the subject matter. His
father sent him a complimentary sample, and for
a while they'd be lying around in the flat. Then, on
Friday morning at the latest, he places one in his
briefcase. At which time he knows nothing of Stoll's
quarrel with Walling, or the possible consequences
to himself.' Gently rocked forward. 'Which almost
gives you the impression that Stoll's murder was in
the pipe-line anyway.'

Metfield gazed at him. 'But why, sir?'

Gently gestured. 'We'd like to know! Whether it
was connected with what happened here, or whether
that just made a convenient occasion. If there was a
plot to murder Stoll going—perhaps, in the beginning, just a gruesome game—then the explosion between Stoll and Maryon Britton would offer an attractive opportunity to act it out. From that point
of view, Stoll's subsequent row with Walling may
even have been an embarrassment to the plotters,
but it made Stoll's removal an urgent matter for
Webster, so there would be no question, then, of not
carrying it out. The pamphlet came out of the briefcase, and Stoll was sent on his way.'

'But Jesus!' Metfield gaped. 'Could it have started as a game?'

'A touch of the real,' Gently said ironically. 'Turner seems to have some such notion. And it would fit what we've seen of Webster—and what we know of the creed he was raised on. Killing Stoll would be the biggest kick, the way-out touch. It would fit.'

'But, great heavens!' Metfield goggled. 'Then perhaps there's a whole crew in it with Webster?'

'One,' Gently said. 'One is my guess. Webster is too bright to share it with more.'

'It—it couldn't be Turner?'

Gently swivelled the chair till he was facing the open window. He stared through it into the yard, his broad features empty of expression. At last he nodded.

'I'm afraid it could. The job would most likely have been done from this end. And Turner is the most likely person to have done it, because he is a youngster who might go along with Webster. Keynes never would, nor Maryon Britton. There's a slight question-mark against Jennifer Britton. But Turner is material that Webster could have worked on. And when we put him under pressure, he came out with Webster's name.' He steepled his fingers. 'But there's one thing against it.'

'Webster was trying to sell him to us,' Metfield said.

'Yes. In fact, my reading is that he came down here for that special purpose. At first, I thought he might have seen Turner this morning, have become aware that Turner posed a threat to him. But the timing prevented that. Webster set out from London before Turner could be expected to get there. No: the reason had to be other. Webster must have summed the case up, just as we did. He realized that Turner was the strongest suspect, so he came down here to give our suspicions a hand.' Gently hesitated. 'Or did he?'

'Pardon, sir?' Metfield gulped.

Gently pulled a face. 'Webster's a clever chummie. He might have foreseen this situation.' He idled the chair for a moment. 'We put pressure on Turner, and eventually Turner drops Webster's name. But Webster has a foolproof alibi, and we have insufficient evidence to proceed against Turner. So now Webster plays a double bluff by appearing to lead us back to Turner. Thus the situation is thoroughly confused. Especially with other valid suspects on the sidelines.'

Metfield took a big swallow of his tongue. 'But look, sir—Webster didn't know we could tie him in with the pamphlet!'

'No, he didn't,' Gently said. 'We shouldn't have discovered that. It's given him an unwelcome new angle to cope with. Because, before, if we had happened to break Turner, it would have been simply his word against Webster's. But now Webster is tied in, Turner's story would have support. What would you expect Webster's reaction to be to that?'

'He'd keep shoving Turner at us,' Metfield said. 'Making like he was innocent, and Turner a villain.'

'Which is what he did,' Gently said. 'And what he will keep doing. We can expect further action from him to that effect.' He grinned at Metfield. 'So we let him go—to dig himself in a little deeper. And meanwhile we'll have the patrols looking out for Turner, because we want him in this office the moment he shows.'

'Yes, sir,' Metfield said. 'I'll pass the word.'

'Turner is Webster's weakness,' Gently said. '*That's* what Webster told *us*.'

He picked up the phone and spun off a number. Metfield gulped and went out to advise control. Gent-

ly cradled the phone under his chin and began filling his pipe while he waited.

'Get me Inspector Lyons.'

The pipe was lighted before Lyons arrived at the
other end. He was chewing something: had probably
been wrested from a lunchtime snack in the canteen.

'Yes, sir?'

'Listen,' Gently said. 'Webster's acquaintances. Tell
me what you've come up with.'

'Well, they're a comic lot, sir,' Lyons masticated.
'In fact, I've copped one for possession of heroin.
Those I've talked to are on the fringe of show business, mostly in and out of work, dressed in gear, talking pop-slang, and proper insolent to policemen. I'd
say there was something amusing going on there, sir,
a bit of nastiness I couldn't place. I took particulars
of one or two of them. I reckon they can stand watching.'

'Were any of them acquainted with Stoll?'

'Two of them said they'd worked with him, sir.
Brian Jeffs, calls himself a singer, and James Fletton,
who paints scenery.'

'What were they doing at the weekend?'

'Jeffs says he was singing in a club, sir. Fletton was
holed up with two birds. I didn't know if you wanted
it checked.'

Gently shrugged to himself. 'Better check those
two. Did you notice if they had transport?'

'Jeffs has a Honda scooter, sir. Fletton I was talking
to in a pub.' He paused to masticate. 'Getting back
to Webster, sir. Seems he may have had someone staying at his flat. I caught the roundsman on second delivery. Webster has taken extra milk during the past
month.'

Gently grunted—that joke again! 'It could be just
that he's developed ulcers.'

'Well, sir, he must have found a lightning cure, because he was back to a pint on Monday.'

'Monday?'

'Yes, sir.'

Gently brooded. The hypothetical lodger would have been there at the weekend. A lodger would make a better alibi than a phone call, yet Webster hadn't mentioned a lodger. Why?

'We have no evidence other than the milkman's?'

'No, sir. It was just an odd inquiry.'

'Nobody seen coming or going with Webster?'

'I've had nobody mentioned to me, sir. The flat is a bit isolated, above a warehouse. There's nobody handy who might have an eye on it. But maybe it's like you say, and he was just trying out a new brand of muesli.'

'Maybe, maybe,' Gently said.

'I was planning to see Walling this afternoon, sir,' Lyons said hastily. 'The Fraud Squad were with him all this morning, and I reckon he's about ripe for a cough.'

'Great,' Gently said. 'But he'll have to wait. The suspense will doubtless do him no harm. What I want to know is whether Webster did have a lodger, and if so, where I can lay hands on him.'

'Yes, sir,' Lyons said glumly. 'I see, sir.'

'Also,' Gently said, 'while you're on your round, ask if anyone knows Lawrence Turner, and whether he is often seen in town.'

'Yes, sir,' Lyons said. 'Could he have been Webster's lodger?'

'I wouldn't think it probable,' Gently said. 'But don't let me prejudice you. What we want to establish is whether Turner knows Webster better than he says.'

He gave Lyons a *portrait parlé* of Turner, and details of the Rosenberg phone call for checking; then he hung up and relit his pipe, which, on an empty stomach, was tasting harsh. Metfield re-entered.

'I've alerted the patrols, sir. They'll pick up Turner when he enters the manor.' He lumped down on a chair. 'So what do we do now, sir?'

'Wait,' Gently said. 'Just wait.'

But when Metfield's phone, screened from routine calls, rang very late in the afternoon, it was still not to bring them news of Turner's reappearance in the area. The local man, who took the call, listened for some moments with a blank expression; then he covered the receiver with his hand and stared uncertainly at Gently.

'Sir. They've got Walling in reception.'

'Walling!'

'Yes, sir. He wants to see you.'

Gently stared too. 'But he should be in town. I can't see the Fraud Squad letting him roam.'

'Well, he's here, sir,' Metfield said. 'He just drove up five minutes ago. Seems he's in a bit of a sweat. I reckon he must have cut and run for it.'

Gently shook his head bemusedly. 'Ask them to send him in,' he said.

Metfield spoke into the phone. After a short interval, a constable ushered in an agitated Walling.

Catching sight of Gently, Walling darted to him and grabbed his arm with trembling hands. He bobbed a tearful face towards Gently's.

'Please!' he sobbed. 'You *must* help me, Superintendent!'

Gently released his arm with some difficulty and took his seat at Metfield's desk. Metfield slid into his old place at the table and quietly reached for pad and pencil. Walling blubbered.

'Sit down, Mr Walling.'

Walling blindly fumbled for a chair and sank on
it. He looked messy. His crumpled plump features
were puffed and greyly pallid. His fluffy hair was
damp and tousled, as though it hadn't seen a comb
that day, and there were dark patches of sweat in the
armpits of his mauve shirt. His hands were grimy:
and some of the grime was getting transferred to his
cheeks.

Gently considered him for a moment.

'Aren't you required in London, Mr Walling?'

'Oh yes—yes!' Walling snivelled haplessly, his fists
scrubbing his swollen eyes.

'Then why are you here?'

'I—I had to come!'

'I don't think I can help you in your affair.'

'Oh yes, you must—please, you must!'

'I'm afraid it's in the hands of a different department.'

Absurdly, Walling tumbled down off the chair and
came shuffling across to the desk on his knees. He
clutched the edge of it with shaking fingers and tilted
his woebegone face to goggle at Gently.

'You must. You must!'

'Please return to your chair.'

'Yes—yes! It's my last hope.'

'Until you return to your chair we can't discuss it.'

'But you can't—you don't know what it means!'

He hauled himself to his feet, however, and sham-
bled back blubbering to the chair. Sitting there, with
his legs dangling, he looked like some wretched,
gnomish Daruma doll. Gently signalled to Metfield.

'Let's have some tea in.'

Metfield departed on the errand. Gently took some
pulls on a cold pipe, then folded his arms and leaned
them on the desk.

'Now! What's it all about?'

Walling gave a sighing moan. 'I'm ruined—did you know that? Ruined!'

'Well,' Gently shrugged. 'That can't be such a shock. You were always running close to the wind with Torotours.'

'But it need never have happened!' Walling sobbed. 'I could have worked it out if they'd given me time. They don't understand. It's a matter of figures. All they know about is cash in the bank!' He howled like a child. 'It's so unfair! At least they could ask someone who knows the business. If you ran things the way they say you should, we'd all be bankrupt by tomorrow morning!'

'There are certain rules,' Gently said.

'Yes, but not like that,' Walling sobbed. 'You can't run finance like a sweet-shop. It's a matter of figures —and—and—confidence!' He howled afresh. 'And they don't understand! They think striking a balance is the only answer. So they say I'm bankrupt, that I'm a rogue—that I'll go inside for twenty years!'

Gently shook his head. 'Not for twenty years.'

'Yes—twenty years!' Walling sobbed. 'And I'm *not* a rogue, I'm a financier, a man who can make figures work for people. If that's dishonest, why is it allowed? Why isn't everyone in prison? It's what finance is about, not cash in the bank, so why—why do they pick on me?'

Gently hunched. 'You know you're in a tangle.'

'But that's just what I wasn't!' Walling sobbed. 'It began when *Chairoplanes* failed to click. When Stoll's fifty thousand went down the drain.'

'Yes, but please! That's exactly the point. I could have covered all that in three months.'

'With the take from Torotours?'

'Yes—yes!'

'What made you think you would ever collect it?'

Walling gaped as though he had been prodded, but just then Metfield entered with the tea. He handed a mug to Walling, whose fingers closed round it perilously, and winked as he placed another mug before Gently. Walling, still snivelling, took gulps from his mug. Tea dribbled from a corner of his tremulous mouth.

Gently drank some tea. 'You'll get time,' he said. 'Though it won't be a sentence like twenty years. But we know the facts about Torotours, and you must expect to be punished for that.'

'I can *explain* Torotours! It's all a mistake. Everyone has trouble with the Spanish.'

'No,' Gently said. 'We have the evidence. Torotours was a plain swindle.'

'But you could talk to them for me!'

Gently shook his head. 'I couldn't. And why should I?'

'Because I don't trust them—and I trust you.'

Gently silently sipped tea.

Walling snivelled. 'Then there's no hope,' he wailed. 'I'll be locked up in that dreadful place. For years and years, until I'm old, and all my friends have forgotten me.' He sobbed. 'And when I come out, destitution and the gutter. And Nina perhaps on the streets, her career ruined by my disgrace.'

Gently grimaced. 'Cheer up! It can't be quite so black as you're painting it.'

'Yes,' Walling sobbed. 'There'll be nothing left for me. It would be best if I died now.'

'You'll get remission and a soft job. They'll probably stick you in the library.'

Walling wagged his head inconsolably and wept tears into his tea.

Gently sighed and reached for the phone. 'I'll give the Yard a ring,' he said. 'They'll be wondering where you've vanished to, and perhaps want you back with an escort.'

'Oh please—no!'

'But I must,' Gently said. 'You don't seem to understand your position.'

'No—it's not important! That's why I've come to you. The fraud doesn't matter any longer.'

Gently rested his hand on the phone. 'Go on,' he said.

Walling's mouth was trembling uncontrollably. 'I—I —didn't tell you the t-truth,' he stammered. 'About last weekend. I w-wasn't in Brighton!'

Gently sat very still, and the silence was echoing. 'Where did you go then?' he said at last.

'To a l-little hotel, out Epping way. It was me who d-did it, who killed Adrian!'

Then another silence—but broken this time by the sudden, furious scuffle of Metfield's pencil. Walling, having delivered his bombshell, sat holding his breath, his pale eyes staring horrifiedly at Gently. In front of his mouth he held the mug, as though to hide that organ of betrayal. His eyebrows were arched so high that they were partly lost under his wayward hair.

Gently drank, and drank again.

'Do you want to tell me about it?' he said.

Walling gulped epileptically behind the mug. 'Yes . . . yes! I'll tell you everything.'

'Take your time,' Gently said.

'I did it,' Walling said. 'I followed him out there. I waited on a layby on the A11, then picked him up as he came by.'

'You knew where he was going?'

'Yes—yes! He'd talked about it the previous weekend. And I knew the place, Mogi's Belt, because we'd been there before, on a picnic.'

'But still, you tailed him there?'

'Yes! I had to make sure he would go as planned.
And then, of course, I waited till he had turned in
and gone to sleep. Then I did it.'

'Where did you wait?'

'Oh, in the forest.'

'I would like to know whereabouts in the forest.'

'Yes, it was a layby, a picnic spot. Somewhere just
off the road.'

'Which road is that?'

'Well—you know, the road! It goes through the
forest to West Brayling. Well, there. It's a sort of car
park, a place to pull off. That's where I waited.'

'Next to Mogi's Belt?'

'Yes, next to it. So I wouldn't have far to carry
the bottle.'

'You could show me the spot?'

'Well—yes. But it was dark. I couldn't be certain.'

'How long did you wait there?'

Walling jiffled the mug. 'It must have been an hour
or two. Or longer. I had to give him time to do his
filming, then pack up and go to bed. I couldn't see
him, of course, from the car, and he might have
spotted me if I'd gone closer. Perhaps it was three
hours. Or nearer four. I know I gave him plenty of
time.'

'And then?'

'Well, I did it.'

'Perhaps you'll expand on that, Mr Walling.'

'Yes—yes.' Walling licked his lips, then took a
quick swig from the mug. 'I had the bottle and the
hose in the boot. So I carried them through the trees
to the caravette. Then I connected the hose to the bottle, led it through a window, and turned on the tap.'

'You led it through a window?'

'Yes, well, a window.'

'Was the the roof of the caravette up or down?'

Walling's free hand strayed to his hair. 'It was dark, you see, I don't think I noticed. Probably up, that would be usual. Though he may have slept with it down. But then, I was nervous. I just pushed the hose in, turned on the tap, and ran off.'

'What colour was the hose?'

'The—the hose?'

'Yes. We have the hose and the bottle on the premises.'

Walling dragged at his hair. 'It was just a cheap hose—I bought it with the bottle, at a branch of Halfords.'

'But the colour?'

'Well, they're all one colour—black, green, even red. I bought two yards—three, it may be. I know I paid fifty pence.'

'You were perhaps too nervous to notice the colour?'

'Yes. Yes. Too nervous.'

'Or the colour of the bottle?'

'No . . . wait! The bottle was either blue or green.'

'But not white?' Gently said.

Walling's fingers tightened. 'Perhaps . . . yes, you could call it white. Or white with some other colour. I really was very nervous.'

Gently drank more tea. Walling, agitatedly, did likewise. Metfield's pencil, which had begun so merrily, had ceased to rustle some time earlier. Now he sat staring blankly at Gently, who sat staring meditatively into his mug. After some moments, Gently set down the mug and reached again for the phone.

'Yes,' he said. 'So I'll just ring to find out if they want you with an escort.'

'B-but,' Walling stammered. 'It's you who want me! I've just m-made a full confession.'

'Sorry,' Gently said. 'It was a brave try.'

'But it's true. I did kill Adrian!'

'You went to Brighton.'

'N-no! I was here.'

'Sorry again,' Gently said.

He began dialling. Walling jumped off his chair and darted furiously to the desk.

'Stop it!' he cried. 'It's all a m-mistake. You'll be sorry for this in a minute!'

'Sit down,' Gently said.

'I w-won't! What I've said is a death-bed confession. Listen—I, Oscar Walling, killed Adrian Stoll. Those are my very last words!'

A podgy hand dived into his hip pocket and came out clutching a small automatic. He jammed it against his head. It clicked feebly. Walling fell down in a faint.

At least, he gave the impression of a faint: but it lasted only till Metfield knelt over him and began slapping his cheeks. Then he wailed and struggled to sit up, his mouth drooling and his eyes aghast. Metfield propped him untenderly against the desk, where he sat gaping and moaning. Gently meanwhile had picked up the gun. It was a .22 Browning. It was loaded.

'Do you have a licence for this?'

'I—I . . . no!'

'Where did you get it?'

'Ugh—ugh—a friend . . .'

'Right. I'm arresting you on an offensive weapons charge.' Gently toyed with the gun. 'Or is that what you wanted?'

Walling swallowed wretchedly. 'I—I killed Adrian! That was a death-bed confession.'

'Oh no it wasn't.'

'I was going to kill myself!'

'Then why did you leave the safety-catch on?'

'I—I forgot . . .'

Gently clicked his tongue. 'You wouldn't have forgotten if you'd meant it. People who really mean to commit suicide don't have elementary lapses of memory. Did Webster give you this gun?'

'No!'

'We shall find out anyway. You may as well tell us.'

'No. Oh please, no!' Walling sank his face in his hands and sobbed.

Gently sat on the chair which Walling lately had occupied and studied the wretched financier. Walling, in his grief, was a comic figure, and not the less so because the grief was genuine. That was his tragedy. If Walling had been a woman, who would have found his tears comic?

'Listen,' Gently said. 'I think you could help me. I'm certain you know who killed Stoll. What you've just done was rather foolish, but I can understand you doing it.'

Walling wailed desolately. 'It was m-me!'

'No,' Gently said. 'It wasn't you. But you thought that since you were ruined anyway, and going to prison, you might as well confess to this too. Well, that's understandable, but it didn't work, and your attempting it raises a question—who were you trying to shield? Who is important enough to you for that?'

'Oh no, no!' Walling wailed. 'It's all a mistake, and I did it!'

'It has to be your daughter.'

'Please, please, no!'

'Then who else?'

'I! I did it!'

And he howled like a great boy, with tears leaking through his pudgy fingers.

The phone rang: Metfield picked it up. 'It's Keynes, sir,' he said.

Gently rose and went to the desk and took the phone from Metfield. 'Yes?'

'I think you'd better come over,' Keynes said. 'Something a little disturbing has happened here. 'It's about Lawrence. We've had a telegram. I think he may not be coming back tonight.'

'He said that?'

'More or less. But I think you had better see it for yourself.'

'Where are you?'

'At the Lodge.'

'Right,' Gently said. 'I'll be over.'

He hung up, and stood a moment staring down at the blubbering Walling. Then he nodded to Metfield.

'Get him up,' he said. 'I think he may as well come too.'

12

They took the Wolseley. Metfield drove; Walling
lolled by himself in the back. He had stopped crying
now and was just looking stupefied, his pale eyes staring wide at nothing. He had made no objection to being taken to Brayling, had let them move him around
like a zombie: you pushed him, and he went. Impossible to guess what he was thinking.

'Do you reckon we're back with Turner, sir?' Metfield murmured, as they left the town limits and sped
towards Brayling.

Gently grunted. 'We're back with nothing! It's
more a question of how many.'

Metfield nodded to the rear seat. 'He could have
been one. And now his conscience is biting him.'

Gently grunted again, but said nothing. Metfield
shrugged and gunned the Wolseley.

They reached the Lodge. Keynes was waiting for
them; he came across as they parked. His eye fell on
the dazed Walling, who showed no sign of recogni-
tion.

'Hullo! What's he doing here?'

Gently gave him a look. 'Does his presence bother
you?'

Keynes shook his head doubtfully. 'Not really.
Though he looks as though he needs a brandy. I suppose you don't have any news of Lawrence?'

'That's what I've come to get from you.'

'Just asking,' Keynes said quietly. 'Your facilities for newsgathering are better than mine.'

He led them inside—Gently first, then the shambling Walling, urged by Metfield. In the drawing-room they found Maryon Britton and her daughter, who was lying on the sofa. Maryon Britton was seated beside her, but she rose quickly as they entered. She stared blankly at Walling for a moment, then moved to confront Gently.

'So all this is nonsense—you've arrested *him*!'

She indicated Walling with a fierce nod. The action and the tone of her voice startled him out of his stupor, and he winced.

'Mr Walling has been helping me,' Gently said.

'Yes, and we all know what *that* means! Good lord, you can see it in his face—he has guilt written all over him.'

'Steady, Maryon,' Keynes murmured.

'No, I'll say what I think!' Maryon Britton said. 'Here they've been hounding poor Lawrence to his wits' end, when they've known all the time who the culprit was. We *told* them who it was—it couldn't have been us!—yet still they persecuted poor Lawrence. And now they've driven him into doing something desperate, just when they've arrested the real killer.' She slipped round Gently to face Walling. 'You did do it, didn't you?' she said. 'It was you who came down here that night, who killed Adrian. Confess it was you!'

'Maryon, Maryon!' Keynes pleaded.

'Go on, confess it!' Maryon Britton cried. 'You may as well, because he'll find out anyway. So be a man for once, and say it.'

Walling was gurgling and rolling his eyes. Now he made a defensive flutter with his hands. 'B-but he won't believe me. He . . . he . . .!' He collapsed on one of the Sheraton chairs.

'You see?' Maryon Britton demanded. 'He *does* confess! And all this business about Lawrence is nonsense.'

'Not if the Superintendent doesn't believe him,' Keynes said. 'And the Superintendent isn't rushing to deny it.'

'That's just his cunning!'

Keynes shook his head. 'I can't quite see Oscar in the role, myself. But I can imagine the old lad trying something Quixotic, and perhaps being too naïve to pull it off.' He flickered a faint smile at Gently. 'Is that the strength of it?'

Gently merely stared. 'Have you reason to think so?'

Keynes shrugged. 'Only knowing my Oscar. Nothing more subtle implied than that.'

'Well, I don't care!' Maryon Britton exclaimed. 'If Oscar has confessed that will do for me. Because I can't see Lawrence in the role, either—and he *hasn't* confessed. He's just being *hounded*.'

'Which is where we came in,' Keynes said. 'Maryon, you'll have to show the Superintendent that telegram.'

'Oh, you've been on his side from the start!' she cried. 'And the telegram is my property, anyway.'

But she flung away, with regal insolence, and crossed to the handsome bureau-bookcase. She returned with a yellow envelope which she dropped contemptuously into Gently's hand.

'There. Now see what you've done!'

The telegram originated from a post office in Chelsea. It had been handed in at four p.m., which was rather more than two hours earlier. The text ran:

I WAS RESPONSIBLE + TRY TO FORGIVE +
GOODBYE + LAWRENCE

It was addressed to Mrs M. Britton, The Lodge, West Brayling.

Gently stared at it: at Maryon Britton.

'Is there a reason why this should have been sent to you?'

'Reason!' she snapped. 'The reason is obvious. He is letting us know that he won't be back.'

'But why send it to you?'

'Why not to me? Haven't I been a mother to him all this time?'

'He's right, Maryon,' Keynes said slowly. 'That telegram would more likely have come to me.'

She stared at him angrily.

'Or Miss Britton,' Gently said.

Jennifer Britton stirred on the sofa. She turned over and sat up, parting the hair from her heavy eyes.

'Lawrence is innocent,' she said dully. '*That's* why he didn't send it to me. He sent it here, but not to me. He couldn't tell *me* he was responsible.'

'Oh, nonsense!' Maryon Britton scoffed.

'Yes,' Jennifer Britton said. 'He couldn't tell *me*. Because it wasn't true. So now I *know* he's innocent. And you and Edwin can think what you like.'

'Oh, what poppycock!' Maryon Britton cried.

'Why would he say what wasn't true?' Gently asked.

'Because,' Jennifer Britton said, 'he knew they thought it, anyway. So he just made it an excuse for not coming back.'

Keynes was looking curiously at Gently. 'Are you thinking what I think you are?' he said. 'It bothered me too, about Maryon getting the telegram, but I've only just begun to realize why.'

'*Wouldn't* he have sent it to you?' Gently said.

'Yes. That's certainly what I have expected. Lawrence has my car, remember, and I'm confident he wouldn't have gone off with that. And if he'd left it somewhere for me to pick up, all the more reason for him to contact me.' He looked steadily at Gently. 'You might almost conclude that Lawrence had forgotten the address of the cottage.'

Gently gave a nod. 'And the style of the telegram?'

'Perhaps a little too tidy,' Keynes said. 'Not so much like Lawrence. Rather more like someone trying to suggest a state of mind.'

'A professional touch.'

'It could be.'

'Look, what *is* this!' Maryon Britton demanded. 'Are you trying to say that the telegram is phoney—that Lawrence didn't send it at all?'

There was a groan from Jennifer Britton.

'May I use your phone?' Gently said.

'Yes—but what in heaven's name is going on!'

'That is beginning to bother me,' Gently said.

The phone was in the hall. Gently rang the Yard and got Lyons's lieutenant, Sergeant Beales. But just then Lyons himself came in, fresh back from a fruitless trip to Campden Hill.

'Walling's skipped!'

Gently reassured him. 'Look. First I want a pick-up on Lawrence Turner. Description you have. Driving Hillman Imp, red, index number EVG 701 H. Repeat back.' Lyons repeated. 'Second a search warrant for Webster's flat. Turner may be there. If not, then most likely in that area.'

'Check,' Lyons said.

There was a spell of harmonics while Lyons passed the instructions to Beales. Then he came back.

'The Rosenberg phone call. That seems to be genuine as far as we've got.'

'Yes,' Gently said. 'I felt it would be. What do we have on Webster's lodger?'

'Nothing positive. A newsagent near the flat describes a hippie character, age about twenty. Seen several times lately in Webster's company. But nothing to show he slept at the flat. Tallish, with a beard.' Lyons paused. 'Doesn't that come near to your description of Turner?'

'Not the hippie bit.'

'He could keep it for town. Have his gear stashed at the flat.'

'Possible,' Gently said. 'But not helpful. We need a lodger who wasn't Turner.'

'A pity,' Lyons said. 'Nothing else on Turner. Nobody I've talked to has seen him around. But then if he was wearing gear and a wig, people might not connect him with our description. What do you think?'

'I think you'd better forget it.'

'Yes,' Lyons said. 'Well, just an idea. Him being tallish, bearded and around twenty. A bit of camouflage is easy these days.' He paused again. 'Any action on Webster?'

'Plenty,' Gently said. 'For a start, a tail. If Turner isn't at the flat I think that Webster can lead us to him. Then I want more detail about Saturday night, when Webster dropped Nina Walling at Campden Hill. The timing. Proof that she really did stay there. Pull in Messiter and grill him.'

'A pleasure,' Lyons said. 'You think she's involved?'

'Walling has given me reason to think so.'

'You want her questioned?'

'No,' Gently said. 'Just get me the facts and sit on them.'

He returned to the drawing-room, where they were sitting in silence, and where Walling was now nursing a glass of brandy. Nobody looked up, except Metfield, who had taken a discreet station by the door. Jennifer Britton had sunk back on the sofa, where she lay with half-closed eyes; her mother sat scowling at Metfield's feet; Keynes was gazing solemnly at his own.

Gently took a chair by the latter.

'Have you given it some thought?'

Keynes slid him a little glance, then shrugged. 'It bothers me as it bothers you. Lawrence wasn't planning a flit this morning.'

'Then what has happened since?'

Keynes shook his head. 'Unless he is playing the same prank as Oscar. Trying to get us off the hook. It would square with Lawrence's character.'

'But you're convinced he wasn't planning it this morning?'

'He wasn't planning it at all!' Maryon Britton broke in. 'That's too ridiculous. It would mean he suspected us. Lawrence isn't stupid enough for that.'

'He was in an odd mood,' Keynes said. 'He didn't want to talk about his session with you. Then you rang this morning and it seemed to decide him. He said there was something he must do in town.'

'Something he must do?'

Keynes nodded. 'Those were the precise words he used. I didn't query it and he didn't explain it. I lent him a couple of pounds for petrol.'

'And that suggests nothing more to you now—like some person he may have been meeting?'

'It doesn't,' Keynes said. 'I wish it did. But I don't know of any acquaintance he had in London.'

Gently grunted. 'He knew Mr Walling. Nina Walling. Ivan Webster.'

Keynes gestured. 'He may have met them down here. But you would scarcely class them as acquaintances.'

'Wouldn't he have seen them in town?'

'Not very likely. He could have run across them when he stayed with Adrian.'

'Or his other trips?'

Keynes looked blank. 'He's been to town only twice in the past year.'

'Because he's living on air,' Jennifer Britton said softly. 'No money for trips. Too proud to borrow.' She turned her face to the sofa. 'Poor Lawry.'

'How much money had he this morning?' Gently asked.

Keynes shook his head. 'Not enough to flit on.'

'He had the car.'

'He wouldn't make off with it. Lawrence is one of those old-fashioned people.'

'So,' Gently said. 'It amounts to this. Turner decided on the trip after I rang. He packed nothing, took little money, and appeared to expect to return today. Instead of which there comes this telegram, containing a confession and saying goodbye.' He turned abruptly to Walling. 'And his acquaintance in London stops with you, your daughter and her lover.' He paused. 'So where is Turner?'

Walling gaped at him, his face sagging. 'I-I—please! H-how should I know? I-I've scarcely ever m-met him!'

'But you know where he is.'

'N-no—!'

'Yes! Turner must have gone to town to see one of you three. He would have missed your daughter and Webster, so that just leaves you.'

'B-but that's insane! I never saw him! I was being q-questioned by detectives.'

'Only in the morning. After that, you were free enough to drive down here.'

'But I didn't see him.'

'Why did you come here?'

Walling dragged on his hair. 'To confess! It's the t-truth, I didn't see Turner. Oh, please, why can't you believe me?'

And suddenly he was on his knees again, with the brandy glass still clasped in his hand. He held it up in a sort of weird supplication, a votive offering to Gently's wrath.

'But at least you would know who *did* see him.'

Walling trembled. 'N-no! Nothing! The d-detectives were with me all the morning. I haven't seen my daughter, or . . . or . . .'

'Look, Webster and your daughter were here earlier.'

Walling shook his head stupidly. 'Please . . . no!'

'Webster was trying to increase my suspicion of Turner—and now, lo and behold! This telegram.'

'I d-don't know anything!'

'Listen. Webster could have sent this telegram. But the telegram would be no use unless Turner had been persuaded not to return here. And Turner hasn't returned here—at least, not yet. All we have is you, with a fake confession. And if you know enough for the need for that, you'll know enough to tell us where to find Turner.'

'But I just d-d-don't!' Walling wailed. 'The telegram, Turner, nothing at all! It's me who's guilty, just me. Oh, I should have shot myself back there!'

He sagged forward, blubbering; and Keynes had to move swiftly to catch the brandy glass from his hand. He helped Walling up, sat him again, and tipped some brandy into his mouth. Walling spluttered and coughed, but drank the brandy; he sat goggling and gaping like a landed fish. Keynes nodded to Gently and went out to the hall. After a moment, Gently followed him.

'I think Oscar's telling the truth,' Keynes said quietly. 'At least, about not having seen Lawrence. If Lawrence has got himself mixed up with Webster, then it must have been Webster he went to see.'

Gently hunched. 'He'd have missed him this morning. Webster couldn't have been back there till after three.'

'So he'd have hung about waiting,' Keynes said. 'Perhaps checked on pubs or coffee-bars that Webster uses. But what the devil did he want with Webster?'

'That's what's troubling me,' Gently said.

'You don't think he was in it with him?'

Gently shook his head. 'But I think he may know more than is good for him. At the end of my questioning he nearly came up with something, as though being under pressure had jolted his memory. But then he seemed to think I wouldn't have believed him. I think he went to town today to check.'

'Something about Webster?'

'That's fairly certain. Have you any idea what?'

Keynes looked blank. 'I know I suggested Webster to you, but I don't really know much about him. I've seen him once or twice down here with Adrian. Seen a couple of sick plays of his on the box. Summed him up as a decadent, and dangerous. That's about all I can tell you of Webster.'

'Turner wasn't attracted to him.'

'Lawrence didn't like him. Felt the same nausea for him that I did.'

'Any letters? Phone calls?'

'None I know of. I assure you, Webster made no impact at all.' He hesitated, his eyes searching Gently's. 'May I ask if you've made up your mind about Webster?'

Gently turned his back on this writer. 'Yes. Since a chat I've had with Walling.'

'But then Lawrence . . . what's happened?'

'I have a pick-up out on Turner.'

'Oh . . . good heavens!' Keynes exclaimed. He dropped down suddenly on one of the hall-chairs.

The telephone rang: Lyons.

'Chiefie, I'm ringing from Webster's flat. Webster as taken off somewhere. His car was seen here earlier, ut not since around four p.m. We're doing our best o make contact.'

'Any sign of Turner or his car?'

'No, sir. Nothing on that yet.'

'Where is Miss Walling?'

'She's at the Capri. Seems she arrived there earlier han usual.'

'What about the flat?'

'We've just made a start, sir. But there's one thing can tell you. Someone's been sleeping on a pull-out ed. It's been folded up with the soiled bed-clothes n it.'

'Hang on,' Gently said.

From the drive outside had come the leisurely runch of wheels on gravel. They passed the house, ircled, and stopped, to the accompaniment of the risk chat of a handbrake. Keynes jumped to his eet: Gently grabbed him. A car door opened and .ammed. Then footsteps sounded in the passage. van Webster entered the hall.

He stared at Gently in mocking surprise, and stood asually flapping his sheepskin jacket.

'Hullo?' Gently said to the phone. 'Forget Webster. Ie's been kind enough to walk through the door.'

13

Webster remained unperturbed. His mocking eye
travelled from Gently to Keynes, then back to Gently.

'Now isn't this just crazy,' he said tauntingly. 'Me
busting two birds with the one shot. I drive down
to see these nice people, and look who I'm running
into as well.'

'What are you doing here?' Gently asked.

Webster fanned the sheepskin. 'Being friendly, fuzz.
Like almost a Good Samaritan I am, driving out here
twice to help my friends. Yah, a Samaritan is what I
am. Before you crash out, ring Ivan.'

'We weren't expecting him,' Keynes said tightly.

'I should have called you,' Webster leered. 'But
like then it would have spoiled a surprise. And my
business being personal, like that.'

Keynes took a step towards him. 'What business?'

'Yah, don't get uptight,' Webster said. 'Haven't I
been saying I'm here to help people? And that goes for
top-brass fuzz, too.' He stroked his lapel. 'So why
don't we go in,' he said. 'What I have to say is for
the benefit of all.'

Keynes glanced at Gently, who shrugged. Keynes
opened the door to the drawing-room. Webster
lounged through. His appearance was greeted by a
whimper from Walling, and an exclamation from
Maryon Britton.

'You!'

Webster ducked his head. Maryon Britton jumped to her feet. She glared aggressively at Webster, who returned the glare with a lazy grin.

'Did you send that telegram?'

'Like which telegram?'

'The one that was supposed to come from Lawrence!'

Webster shook his head in mock wonder. 'Like I tried to talk him out of it. He must have sent it just the same.'

'Then you know where he is?'

Webster nodded towards Gently. 'Maybe not officially or for the record. But maybe, like between friends, I could have a wild notion. Maybe that's why I'm here now.'

Jennifer Britton sat up. 'Where is Lawrence?'

'Around,' Webster said. 'He's around. Do I get to sitting down?'

Maryon Britton's chin tilted. 'Sit,' she said, hissing the word.

Webster chose a chair and sprawled on it. Maryon Britton returned to the sofa. Keynes, tense-faced, drew up a chair till he was sitting almost knee-to-knee with the scriptwriter. Gently quietly closed the door and motioned Metfield nearer to it. Then he crossed to the French windows, closed those too, and took a chair by them.

Webster didn't seem to notice: he sprawled indolently, hands dug into the pockets of the sheepskin.

'Yah, well,' he said. 'This afternoon. I'd just got back from the country scene. So there's this Turner parked outside and waiting to grab me as I came in. Seems like he felt the fuzz were breathing on him, that it was time he busted out. Like he wanted some help from his friends until he wasn't such a hot property.'

'Yes, that's likely!' Maryon Britton snapped. 'When were you such a friend of Lawrence's?'

'Lady, lady!' Webster drawled. 'Who else could that nervy cat turn to? Me, he knew. I put him in the scene when he was on that trip with Adrian. Like it struck him I was no fuzz-lover, wouldn't blow him to the pigs. So he came to Ivan. If you work it out, there was nowhere else for him to go.'

'Yes, but why?' Keynes demanded hotly. 'Lawrence didn't have to run. He wasn't intending to, either, not when he left the cottage this morning.'

Webster leered from under his hair. 'That was this morning, Mack,' he said. 'By mid-afternoon he'd had time to meditate, and like then he decided the Smoke was cosier.'

'That doesn't sound like Lawrence.'

'Be told,' Webster said.

'This lout is lying,' Keynes said to Gently.

'Yah?' Webster said. 'What I'm trying not to say is that Turner knew he had reasons why he should hole up. Well, I don't know that. He didn't tell me. So just you go on believing he's innocent. But meantime there he was on my doorstep, about blowing his lid because of the fuzz.'

He tossed back his hair and stared meanly at Keynes, who was regarding him with still, empty eyes.

'But what happened to Lawrence?' Jennifer Britton said.

Webster relaxed, his eyes hooding. 'Yah, so I took him inside,' he said. 'Made some coffee, tried to cool him down. Like I tried to tell him the fuzz couldn't touch him, like he only needed to keep his cool. But he was too strung up, you couldn't undo him. So I thought it was best to go along.'

'You agreed to hide him?' Keynes said.

Webster sneered. 'Forget it, Mack. Not with the fuzz flapping their ears do I say comic things like that.'

'But you advised him?'

'Yah, I advised him.'

'You know where he is.'

'Lay off,' Webster said. 'You aren't the fuzz, don't make like the fuzz. Let them come up with the square questions.'

'Then what have you come to tell us?'

Webster pushed his face at Keynes. 'I've come to tell you this, Mack, and you'd best grab it. Your blue-eyed boy is, like, very disturbed, and needs to have someone holding his hand. I would have kept him at the flat, but that wasn't sensible, so I gave him some advice and turned him loose. He is going to phone you, and when he does, the smart thing will be to get out there fast. Because he's like to crash out, you comprehend? That phone call will maybe be the last.'

Jennifer Britton came slowly to her feet. She stared hauntedly at Webster. *'You've killed Lawrence.'*

Webster's hands crept out of his pockets. 'Are you stoned?' he jeered. 'More like that cat would have killed me.'

'Yes, you killed him,' Jennifer Britton said. 'I knew you'd killed him when you walked in. I knew that Adrian was going to die. Now I know you've killed Lawrence.'

Webster hesitated fractionally before bursting into harsh laughter. 'This cow is crazy,' he jeered. 'A crazy cow. Like someone should lock this cow up.'

'He killed Lawrence,' Jennifer Britton said. She pointed a straight, untrembling finger. 'He killed him. He killed Lawrence. That man there killed Lawrence.'

'Look!' Webster shouted. 'This is madsville!'

'*Did* you kill him?' Keynes said.

'Like would I have walked in here if I had?'

'Yes,' Jennifer Britton said. 'He killed him. He killed him.'

There came a sudden little whimper from Walling's corner and the plump man struggled to his feet. He, too, pointed a finger at Webster, though in his case the finger was trembling violently. His shapeless mouth wobbled.

'He k-killed Adrian, too!'

'Why, you fat bum-boy!' Webster snarled, leaping up.

'Sit down!' Keynes snapped. 'You'll hear what he says.'

'Yah?' Webster barked. 'He'd better remember his daughter!'

Walling swayed, but his finger kept pointing. 'He killed Adrian,' he said. 'He told me he killed him. He's been asking me for money. He said if I shopped him he would shop Nina, too.'

'You lying bastard!' Webster howled.

'And it's true, isn't it?' Keynes demanded.

'No it isn't! He's lying like a pig.'

'There are two fingers pointing at you, Webster.'

Webster struck at him. Keynes went rolling. Webster bolted towards the door. Metfield moved in front of it: without hesitation, Webster flashed a karate chop at Metfield's throat.

'Oh no you don't, sonny!' Metfield grunted, bobbing away with unexpected agility. Then he hooked Webster with a slamming left shot. Webster went down. He didn't move.

'Oh God, have you killed him?' Maryon Britton cried.

'Just restrained him, ma'am,' Metfield said. He polished his knuckles and looked across at Gently, who was sitting unmoved by the French windows. 'Cuffs, sir?'

Gently nodded.

Maryon Britton laughed a little hysterically. Jennifer Britton was standing stiff and huge-eyed. Walling had collapsed again on his chair.

Metfield snapped cuffs on the still-groggy Webster and heaved him unceremoniously to a seat. The scriptwriter sat massaging his swelling jaw and staring hate at the fleshy Inspector. Gently rose slowly and came over. Webster's flaming eyes hooked on to him. Gently placed a chair to confront Webster and sat, his arms folded.

'Now listen carefully,' he said. 'You are under arrest on suspicion of being involved in the murder of Adrian Stoll. The punishment for murder is life imprisonment, which formerly could be as little as nine-and-a-half years. That is so no longer. It is possible now to give a sentence for a minimum number of years. And if you have made away with the young man, Lawrence Turner, you may never see the outside world again. Do you understand?'

Webster tossed his hair furiously. 'Yah, I understand, fuzz,' he snarled. 'And now you listen to me, because you like can't prove any of it, and you're going to be sorry you ever arrested me. I wasn't around when Stoll was murdered. That call from Rosenberg wasn't a fake. And if that fat pansy says I'm involved, it's just his word against mine, yah? And who's going to believe a twister like that, and him with a motive as big as a house? So you'd just better get this hardware off me, or like I'll pull the roof in on you.'

'Who was your lodger at Battersea?' Gently said.

Webster's eyes flickered. 'Who says I had one?'

'We say it,' Gently said. 'He's been staying with you for several weeks. He got out of your flat only last weekend.'

'That's a lie! There's been nobody there.'

'A youngster of about twenty,' Gently said.

'It's a frame!'

'Described as a hippie type. Tallish. Wears a beard.'

Webster's narrow features writhed. 'You won't get away with this, fuzz,' he snarled. 'There's no connection. You can't connect it. I'm clear all the way along the line.'

'I can't connect it—but Turner can?'

'Just turn me loose!' Webster bawled. 'You'll never get me for doing Turner. That one's as bum as all the the rest.'

'*Because you have an alibi.*'

'Yah—an alibi!'

'Such as coming down here to bring a message.'

Webster came off his chair, his manacled fists clubbed, and was promptly dumped back into it by Metfield.

'You lying bastards!' he roared.

'So this was your alibi,' Gently said. 'You came down here to hint at Turner's impending suicide while your confederate was engaged in murdering him.'

'Prove it!' Webster howled. 'You can't prove it—because like I'm here and nowhere else. And if you're pinning your hopes on Turner, just bloody forget all about it, fuzz.'

'Where is Turner?'

'I said forget it!'

'It could mean the difference between ten and thirty years.'

'Yah, difference nothing,' Webster snarled. 'Because Turner won't talk any more than Adrian—it's all

finished, kaput, in the can. And you've got nothing
to come but grief.'

Gently leaned back, considering him. 'You could
have phoned that message.'

'Then like why didn't I?' Webster snarled.

'And you could have got an alibi at, say, Television
Centre. You didn't have to drive eighty miles.'

Webster's eyes flamed at him. 'And like if that's so,
fuzz?'

'There'd be a reason, wouldn't there?' Gently said.
'A reason like a need for transport waiting at this
end. For someone whose transport had to be ex-
pendable.'

Metfield gave a startled exclamation. 'A carbon copy
—by Jesus, it could be!'

'A confederate,' Gently said. 'Driving a Hillman
Imp. With a passenger. And going where?'

Webster had paled. 'You're crazy, fuzz!'

'Am I?' Gently said, rising. 'When I'm dealing with
one of Dicky Deeming's disciples—who is turning out
as predictable as his master?'

'Yah, you're crazy, crazy!' Webster gabbled. 'There's
nothing out there. Turner's in town.'

'Nothing out where?'

'Like nowhere—nothing!' Webster clattered the
handcuffs like a maniac.

Gently turned to Keynes, who was standing behind
him. 'Come on,' he said. 'I want you with me.'

'Yes—but where?' Keynes queried.

'Mogi's Belt.'

Webster tried to lunge from the chair. Metfield
restrained him.

Gently let Keynes drive the Wolseley, and Keynes
drove it fast. He took the back road from the Lodge
and turned off by the small church.

'Sure this is quickest?' Gently said.

Keynes gave an agitated nod. 'It joins 64, which takes us through. But God, will it be quick enough?'

Gently grunted and picked up the handset.

'Mother calling Control.' Control answered. 'Send an ambulance to Warren Ride. Expected gas poisoning victim. Probably located Mogi's Belt.'

Control responded.

'Further message. Alert patrols to converge on area. Detain suspect of following description, also any other person found in area.' He gave the description. 'Message ends.'

Control confirmed and timed without comment. Then messages began to go out to the patrols: Gently switched off the receiver.

'You're so damned cool!' Keynes muttered. 'Doesn't a kid's life mean anything to you?'

'Just keep driving,' Gently said. 'Not making mistakes is what it means.'

Keynes just drove. They skittered along the ride with its burns of soft sand and scatters of pine needles, past several cross-rides, coming shortly to a junction with a wider track. Keynes turned right.

'64. A sort of north–south spine road.'

'How much further?'

'Most of a mile. The Battle Area is straight ahead.'

He gunned the Wolseley to fifty, which was fast going over the bumpy surface. Sections of Corsican, Scots and larch went flickering by on either hand. They saw nobody and no vehicle. The evening forest appeared deserted. Ride after ride went spoking past, each departing emptily into its own twilight. After all, was this a mistake? A reading fostered by a piece of inspired cunning? When the forest was empty it seemed very empty, as though nobody would ever again set foot there.

Then, ahead, the rusty mesh fencing, with behind it deep undergrowth.

'Now!' Keynes breathed. He slewed left into a boundary track which Gently recognized. But still there was some distance to go, over a surface that reduced the speed to near walking pace. At last a bend, and then the gate. Keynes slammed to a stop and they jumped out. The gate was open: and fresh tracks of car tyres showed in leaf-mould beyond it.

'Easy!' Gently warned. 'We want to catch him.'

'Oh, to hell with that!' Keynes exclaimed.

He raced forward into the underbrush, crashing through the bracken and elders. Gently went too, but holding back, trying to keep the scene under observation. They burst through the honeysuckle and mounted the bank. Below, in the dell, sat the red Hillman.

'Oh, the devils, the devils!' Keynes panted.

Beside the Hillman stood a grey gas bottle. A hose ran from it through the driver's window. In the rear of the car lay a huddled figure.

'Come on—come on!'

Keynes sprinted down the slope. He snatched the hose away from the car. He grabbed the door-handle and yanked; but the door had been left locked.

'Sorry!' Gently panted.

He picked up the bottle and sent it crashing through the window. He heaved the door open, flipped the seat forward, and dragged out the body to tumble on the bracken.

It was Turner, and he was still alive, though he was cherry-faced and snoring. His mouth was sealed with surgical plaster which Gently at once ripped off. His wrists and ankles were bound with Scotch tape and there was a heavy contusion on his scalp. For the rest he seemed uninjured. They had probably got there just in time.

'Do you know mouth-to-mouth resuscitation?'

'Yes.'

'Give it to him.'

Keynes dropped on his knees in the bracken, manipulated Turner's tongue, and began. Gently rapidly checked through the car, expecting and finding nothing. In leaf-mould near it, partial footprints, flat, made probably by a sandal. Then further off another print, leading deeper into the belt. And another. After that, they were lost in bracken and drifted needles.

Chummie, waiting for Turner to die, had retreated into the belt when Gently and Keynes had disturbed him.

There were fresh crashing sounds up above, and two patrolmen came down the slope. They stared at the scene round the car with curious, hard eyes. Gently came back to the car.

'Has the ambulance arrived?'

'Yes, sir. But it can't nicely get up the track. They're bringing a stretcher.'

'How many up there?'

'A couple of cars, sir, and us.'

'A dog?'

'They're sending one, sir.'

Gently nodded to the trees. 'Chummie is in there. You stay here. If he shows, no nonsense. Understood?'

'You bet, sir,' the patrolman said.

Gently departed up the slope. He passed the S.J.A.B. men coming down, one with a rolled stretcher on his shoulder. Jammed in by the gate were the three patrol cars, and a van, which had just arrived.

'Is that the dog?'

'Yes, sir.'

'Take him in. See what he can pick up at the car.'

The dog, a coal-black Alsatian, jumped eagerly from the van and set off enthusiastically with its handler.

'Who is senior man?'

A sergeant stepped forward.

'I want this fence patrolled along its length. If chummie slips over it into the forest we may be hunting him all night. Can you do it?'

'Yes sir, I reckon. I'll put in a call for another dog. We've got patrols towards Brayling and on the Latchford Road. I'd say that would have it covered, sir.'

'Where does Mogi's Belt end?'

'Near Starveacre Farm, sir.'

'Can you get a dog ad two men in at that end?'

The sergeant considered. 'Yes sir, I reckon. It should be safe on this side of the fen.'

He touched a salute and turned to give orders. Two of the cars bumbled off along the track. Gently hurried back to the scene at the car, where the S.J.A.B. men were belting Turner on the stretcher.

Turner's breathing was quieter now, and his colour less hectic, but he showed no sign of returning consciousness. His lips were parted, showing bloodstained teeth: it gave him the macabre aspect of a clubbed rabbit.

'Where are you taking him?'

'Latchford and District.'

Gently beckoned to one of the patrolmen. 'Call in for a man to be stationed at the bedside. Then come back and wait here.'

'Hold on!' Keynes exclaimed. 'I'm going with Lawrence.'

Gently shook his head. 'I want you with me.'

'But why?'

'Because you may be able to identify chummie. I have a notion that you could know him.'

Keynes stared at him oddly. 'Well, if you say so. But Webster's kind and I don't mix.'

'He is probably someone Lawrence knew,' Gently said. 'Someone you could know. I want you along.' He turned to the dog-handler. 'Any luck?'

'No, sir. The gas must have taken off the scent.'

'He can't get it from the footprints?'

'He's had a smell at them, sir. But I wouldn't like to promise too much from that.'

'Right,' Gently said. 'You follow in the line of them. The rest of us, spread out. If chummie tries a break, let the dog go. Otherwise, we pick him up quietly.'

The four of them fanned out across the belt and began to move forward under the trees. The patrolman was on the left flank, nearest the boundary with the Battle Area; then came the dog-handler, then Gently and Keynes. They advanced slowly, having to penetrate an underbrush of bracken, elder and bramble. The dog worked busily, but without direction. After they left the dell there were no more footprints.

They advanced some hundreds of yards up the silent belt.

'Do you think he's still about?' Keynes murmured to Gently.

'He's still about. He had to be waiting here. He couldn't leave Turner with his hands tied.'

'He'd have been watching Lawrence die.'

'What else?'

Keynes shuddered. 'I don't know him. Anyone capable of that I could spot. Webster's the only one I know.'

'Get further over to the fence.'

Keynes veered towards the flank. His face was pale and his mouth tight. Now the dog was working

further to the left, though possibly only on the scent
of a rabbit. The belt was too still. Above, the low
sun was yellow in the tops of the pines. Below there
was dimness in the screens of brush, a promise of an
early, deep twilight. Then the dog set up an ex-
cited growling.

'What's he saying?' Gently said.

'I'm not quite sure, sir. But if he's on the scent,
I'd say that chummie isn't far away.'

But where? The spot they had come to was rather
more open than some parts of the belt. Bracken had
thickly colonized the area and the only underbrush
was low brambles. Along the lip of the belt, where
it dropped steeply to the bogland, the great pines
stood in massive line, but further in they were spaced
widely, which perhaps had encouraged the growth
of the bracken. Yet the dog continued to growl.

'Let him go.'

The handler released him. The dog lifted its muz-
zle, snuffling, emitting growls of deep menace. Then
it took off suddenly, like a black missile, towards
one of the huge pines at the edge of the belt.

'Follow up!'

But before they could obey a figure stepped from
behind the pine. It raised its hand. There was a
crack. The dog went rolling over in the bracken.

'You bastard!' the dog-handler shouted.

'Keep back!' Gently snarled. The gun cracked again.
A bullet smacked into a tree, and a plume of pine
needles drifted down. The man stood for a second
with gun poised, daring them to make a move towards
him; then he jumped back past the tree and down
the slope that bounded the belt.

'Right—keep him in view!'

They pounded through the bracken to the spot
where the man had vanished. He had cleared the slope

and its thickets of gorse and was making plashy tracks
through the bog beyond. He turned to snap another
shot at them.

'I'm going after him, sir!' the dog-handler cried.

'You're not!' Gently rapped. 'That's an order. As
from now he belongs to the Army.'

'But he shot my dog, sir!'

'It's happened before. Nobody is following that
man in there.'

The handler gazed after the gunman with anguished
eyes, then groaned and threw himself down by the
pine tree. Gently looked round for Keynes.

'Well?' he said.

Keynes had the appearance of wanting to retch.
But he nodded his head. 'Yes. I know him. There's a
photograph of him in Adrian's study.'

'Stöll's son?'

'Yes. Marcus.'

'Who collects the better part of Stoll's estate.'

'Yes.' Keynes closed his eyes. 'Oh God almighty. A
parricide.'

Now the figure was wading kneedeep in bog, and
once sank in as far as his waist; but he recovered
energetically to haul himself to firmer going. Then
he was through it, and ploughing up a sand slope
to the cover of stunted birches.

'You stay here,' Gently said to the patrolman.
'Make sure he doesn't double back. And make sure
this officer stays here with you. I don't want any
heroics at all.'

'Yes, sir,' the patrolman said, saluting.

Gently motioned to Keynes and set off for the cars.
But they had gone barely a dozen yards when there
was a soft, almost leisurely explosion from the distance
of the Battle Area.

'Sir—sir!' the patrolman shouted.

They hastened back to where he was stationed.

From among the small birches across the bogland a tendril of grey smoke was loitering into the air.

'He . . . he must have kicked into a mine, sir!'

The explosion was followed by complete silence. The grey smoke unrolled in the evening sky and slowly vanished. Then there was nothing.

14

Marcus Stoll died with a receipt for a bottle of gas in his pocket. A second receipt was found among his possessions in a rented room in Westbridge Road. Found also was a letter from his mother, expressing pleasure that he was staying with her 'old friend Ivan', and warning him to keep away from his father 'to avoid disillusioning the old square'. From the letter it was plain that Stoll's provision for his son was familiar ground to both writer and reader.

Thus Turner's statement would scarcely have been necessary to incriminate Marcus Stoll, but it formed the basis of charges against Webster calculated to double his effectual sentence. It related how Turner, visiting London as Stoll's guest, had spent an evening with Webster and his followers, among whom had been an American, known as 'Chuck,' who was staying at Webster's flat. Turner had felt there was something familiar about 'Chuck', but at the time he could not decide what, and it was not until his memory had been spurred by the shock of suspicion that he connected 'Chuck' with the photograph in Stoll's study. Even then the identification had seemed farfetched, and he hadn't dared to mention it to Gently; instead he had sought to verify it by a further meeting with 'Chuck'. Unfortunately, 'Chuck' divined his purpose. Turner found him alone in Webster's flat; 'Chuck' invited him in, gave him a drink, then coshed him from behind and bound and gagged him. Several hours passed before Webster returned, when there was a conversation which Turner didn't hear; but eventually Webster had helped 'Chuck' to load Turner into the Imp, and to cover him over with a rug. There followed a conversation which Turner did hear. Webster spoke of 'setting it up' with a telegram. He arranged a pick-up spot with 'Chuck' at the junction of the road and Warren Ride. Following a short further interval, presumably when 'Chuck' went out to buy the bottle and hose, Turner was driven to the forest and his presumed suicide set in motion. The effect of the gas was watched with interest by 'Chuck'; but he departed just as Turner was losing consciousness.

No case was offered against Nina Walling, who was almost certainly an accessory after the fact of Stoll's death; while the fraud charge against her father subsequently foundered on a curious technicality. Only the offensive weapons charge stuck: Walling was fined one hundred pounds.

The trial required Gently's presence in the district, and he paid a visit to Keynes before returning to London. He found the writer packing gear into the blue-and-white Dormobile, which stood polished and handsome in his cottage drive. Keynes came out smilingly to greet Gently.

'Does this suggest unusual callousness?' he grinned.

Gently ghosted a shrug. 'A van is a van. And we only live in the present moment. Are you off somewhere?'

Keynes nodded happily. 'Off to Scotland in the morning. Maryon has rented a cottage at Balquhidder. They've taken Lawrence and gone already.'

'To get him away from it all.'

'Yes. It's been a ghastly time for Lawrence.'

'Lawrence is young.'

Keynes pulled a face. But the smile had left his eyes for a moment.

'I didn't see much of you in court,' Gently said.

'Did you expect to?' Keynes asked.

Gently hesitated. 'Perhaps not. Though it should have interested a student of human nature.'

Keynes shook his head. 'This came too close. I had seen all I wanted in Mogi's Belt. Now I want to forget it, if forgetting's possible, to try not to think of those things again.' He glanced quickly at Gently. 'Do you forget them?'

'I'm a tough professional,' Gently shrugged. 'I have a case waiting in Kent at the moment. A rape and strangling. It doesn't stop.'

'No, it doesn't stop,' Keynes said sombrely. 'Something's chronically rotten in the state of Denmark. A disease of egoism, I think. A false imagining of self.' He perched on the Dormobile's step. 'Do you believe there's a direction to reality?' he said. 'A progressive motion towards love, and a retrogressive motion towards hate?'

Gently hitched up a folding stool and also sat. 'What do you call reality?' he said.

'Aha,' Keynes said. 'The stubborn question. It has baffled philosophers since before the Flood. The Buddhists describe reality as Essence of Thought, and the physicists as patterns of energy. The metaphysicians have come up with noumenon, an excessively unsatisfactory concept.'

'But you?' Gently said.

Keynes stroked his chin. 'Yes, I do have a theory,' he said. 'After staring at a wall for thirty years, like a latter-day Bodhidharma.'

'Which wall was that?'

'It was Descartes's proposition, which involves a fallacy of unexpected proportions. It supposes we

are split into simultaneous selves, and that one self
is conscious of the acts of the other. Which of course
is nonsense. The proposition should run: I *thought*,
therefore I *was*. And that's what I stared at for thirty
years, without seeing what lay on the other side of
it.'

'Go on,' Gently said.

Keynes grinned fiendishly. 'The other day I bought
a pad of coarse manuscript paper. I wanted to see if
it would take pen-and-ink, so I scribbled down my
criticism of Descartes. The pen flowed nicely, and I
went on writing, letting the criticism casually expand.
Then, a few lines later, there it was—the country on
the other side of the wall.'

'Well?' Gently said.

Keynes pulled out a notebook. 'Here's the defini-
tive statement,' he said. 'Of course, I should bury it
in reams of turgid prose, but it seems a pity to inter
anything so simple.' He read from the notebook:

> Time, space and being are not independent es-
> sences of reality, but merely arbitrary concepts
> which we have imposed upon it for practical
> purposes. The essence of reality, to which they
> refer, is motion; motion *is* reality, and reality
> consists in motion. All duration, extension and
> phenomena arise from motion alone. Further-
> more, motion is single, and indivisible into cate-
> gories of mental and physical.

He closed the notebook. 'That's it in a nutshell. Motion and reality are interchangeable terms. At this
point the Void of the Buddists and the physicist's
energy-patterns coincide, while the door is slammed
on metaphysics, which have had their clothes stolen.'

Gently stirred the gravel with his foot. 'And in
this motional reality you see a direction?'

'Yes, of course—a moral direction: a direction from hate to love.'

'In which a false image of self is retrogressive?'

'Yes, the egoistic disease. By pursuing the false image we are running contra to reality.'

'So what cure do you propose?'

Keynes smiled. 'I shall have to stare at my wall again. And in the meantime refer you to the dharmas, with which the theory brings you into accord.' He rose from the step. 'Shall I make some tea?'

'If it doesn't run contra,' Gently said.

Keynes chuckled. He pointed to the van. 'There's something that never will,' he said. 'If motion is the style of reality, travelling is the style of man. And thanks to Adrian, I have the instrument. I don't think the poor fellow will haunt me.'

The police-dog that died was called Nero, and the Belt was re-named in his memory. But still the Forestry failed to get permission to thin the great pines. When the Trail pamphlet was reprinted all mention of the badgers was deleted; and at night they continued, in their habit of centuries, to cross the small dell and enter the trees.

The National Bestseller!

GOODBYE, DARKNESS

by WILLIAM MANCHESTER

author of *American Caesar*

The riveting, factual memoir of WW II battle in the Pacific—
and of an idealistic ex-marine's personal struggle to understand
its significance 35 years later.

"A strong and honest account, and it ends with a clash of
cymbals."—*The New York Times Book Review*

"The most moving memoir of combat in World War II that I
have read. A testimony to the fortitude of man. A gripping,
haunting book."—William L. Shirer

A Dell Book   **$3.95**   **(13110-3)**

Dell Bestsellers

- [ ] **NOBLE HOUSE** by James Clavell..............$5.95 (16483-4)
- [ ] **PAPER MONEY** by Adam Smith................$3.95 (16891-0)
- [ ] **CATHEDRAL** by Nelson De Mille..............$3.95 (11620-1)
- [ ] **YANKEE** by Dana Fuller Ross....................$3.50 (19841-0)
- [ ] **LOVE, DAD** by Evan Hunter......................$3.95 (14998-3)
- [ ] **WILD WIND WESTWARD**
  by Vanessa Royal $3.50 (19363-X)
- [ ] **A PERFECT STRANGER**
  by Danielle Steel $3.50 (17221-7)
- [ ] **FEED YOUR KIDS RIGHT**
  by Lendon Smith, M.D. $3.50 (12706-8)
- [ ] **THE FOUNDING**
  by Cynthia Harrod-Eagles...........................$3.50 (12677-0)
- [ ] **GOODBYE, DARKNESS**
  by William Manchester................................$3.95 (13110-3)
- [ ] **GENESIS** by W.A. Harbinson.....................$3.50 (12832-3)
- [ ] **FAULT LINES** by James Carroll $3.50 (12436-0)
- [ ] **MORTAL FRIENDS** by James Carroll $3.95 (15790-0)
- [ ] **THE SOLID GOLD CIRCLE**
  by Sheila Schwartz $3.50 (18156-9)
- [ ] **AMERICAN CAESAR**
  by William Manchester................................$4.50 (10424-6)

At your local bookstore or use this handy coupon for ordering:

Dell DELL BOOKS
P.O. BOX 1000, PINE BROOK, N.J. 07058-1000

Please send me the books I have checked above. I am enclosing $ _____ (please add 75c per copy to cover postage and handling). Send check or money order—no cash or C.O.D.'s. Please allow up to 8 weeks for shipment.

Mr./Mrs./Miss _____

Address _____

City _____ State/Zip _____